KU-242-402

THE SCARS OF IRON EYES

Hot on the trail of outlaw Two Fingers McGraw, bounty hunter Iron Eyes realizes that he is headed into the forest where he grew to manhood. Most of the woodland has been felled, there is a war going on between two rival outfits for the remainder — and now their guns are turned on him! Stuck in the middle of a deadly battle, Iron Eyes seeks refuge in the trees from the enemies who are eager to add to his scars . . .

Books by Rory Black
in the Linford Western Library:

THE FURY OF IRON EYES
THE WRATH OF IRON EYES
THE CURSE OF IRON EYES
THE SPIRIT OF IRON EYES
THE GHOST OF IRON EYES
IRON EYES MUST DIE
THE BLOOD OF IRON EYES
THE REVENGE OF IRON EYES
IRON EYES MAKES WAR
IRON EYES IS DEAD
THE SKULL OF IRON EYES
THE SHADOW OF IRON EYES
THE VENOM OF IRON EYES
IRON EYES THE FEARLESS

RORY BLACK

---◆---

THE SCARS OF IRON EYES

Complete and Unabridged

LINFORD
Leicester

First published in Great Britain in 2013 by
Robert Hale Limited
London

First Linford Edition
published 2015
by arrangement with
Robert Hale Limited
London

Copyright © 2013 by Rory Black
All rights reserved

A catalogue record for this book is available
from the British Library.

ISBN 978–1–4448–2462–9

Published by
F. A. Thorpe (Publishing)
Anstey, Leicestershire

Set by Words & Graphics Ltd.
Anstey, Leicestershire
Printed and bound in Great Britain by
T. J. International Ltd., Padstow, Cornwall

This book is printed on acid-free paper

*Dedicated to my California
friend Karla Buhlman*

Prologue

The shimmering heat haze hung to the south of Silver Creek as though it were guarding the remote settlement from uninvited intruders. Yet it would take more than hot moving air to stop the most determined of souls. At first no one even saw the approaching horseman beyond the noisome mist but slowly the image of horse and rider came together to form a chilling apparition. There were few sights in the West which conjured up a more frightening image than the one of the infamous bounty hunter seated astride the magnificent palomino stallion. There was a stark contrast between mount and master. The horse was handsome and the rider was the most hideous-looking of men. The long limp mane of matted hair flapped on the horseman's wide shoulders like the

1

wings of a black bat. Yet for those who were unlucky enough to focus briefly upon the scarred features of the man's face the long hair that fell across his distinctive countenance acted as a mask. Every last fight and battle seemed to be carved into the mutilated face of the rider.

A concerted gasp greeted him everywhere he went, but he had grown deaf to it. His horrific appearance brought both revulsion and sympathy from those who set eyes upon it. It was easy to see why so many feared him. Men of all colours and creeds always fear what they do not understand or what simply looks different from themselves.

Dust floated across the path of the horseman as he steered his powerful palomino towards the array of weathered buildings. Only his mane of black hair seemed to move as he sat astride his high-shouldered horse. Yet, although he looked as if he were staring straight ahead, his eyes were darting back and forth, searching for the gun which he knew would one day fire the fatal bullet and end his wanderings.

Those who managed to drag their eyes from the strange and disturbing sight of the bounty hunter suddenly noticed something about his handsome horse. It was limping. Limping badly but still obeying the commands of the rider with the sharp spurs who sat on the ornate Mexican saddle.

The magnificent animal was lame, yet its master remained on his high perch, like a vulture waiting for something to die.

The scattering of wooden and red-brick buildings were probably not deserving of being called a town in the true sense of the word. Half the buildings looked abandoned and those which were still occupied seemed on the verge of collapse. This was a ghost town waiting to happen and the horseman knew it.

He had been here before and recalled what it had looked like on that visit. Like so many other towns it had grown up quickly when silver had been discovered. As with so many near-abandoned towns its original life source had probably petered out.

He had travelled far and wide over the years before returning to this place, which he remembered from long before his reputation had become infamous. The last time he had ridden down its main street it had been bustling with activity.

Now it just seemed dead or at least to be waiting to die.

Iron Eyes tilted his head and stared through the strands of limp hair at the one façade he always sought out. The saloon was still in business and that was what he considered important.

There were a handful of people moving around the dust-caked settlement. Everyone looked as though they too were just waiting for the Grim Reaper to call and put them out of their misery.

Yet the rider drew the attention of every one of them.

Perhaps it was because he showed his handsome mount no mercy, as most men would do when their horse was lame. He stayed in his saddle and continued to thrust his spurs backwards to encourage the horse to continue limping forward.

Maybe it was because he showed little sign of animation in his long thin form. He remained virtually unmoving apart from the rocking of his boots as they kept on jabbing into the palomino's flesh.

There was another more haunting reason why so many of the town's ancient people could not take their eyes from the rider as he slowly passed them.

It was the memory of when they had first seen him. Not now, but long ago when they had all been younger. Yet apart from Iron Eyes having more scars upon his face he himself did not appear to have aged. He remained the same as if he had made a pact with the Devil never to grow older, as they all had done.

Another memory filled each of the onlookers' hearts and that was how dangerous he was. They had seen how he could kill all those years ago. How there was no hint of any charity in his dark soul. Iron Eyes killed with a cold precision that none of the elderly townsfolk had been able to forget.

This was not just a man whom they watched.

It was the return of a nightmare.

You do not forget a nightmare as easily as a dream.

That one brief but bloody encounter, which every person watching the bounty hunter had witnessed was carved into their very souls. No mere nightmare could ever have equalled it.

Dust rolled across the street, taking a bundle of dried tumbleweed with it as the horseman at last drew rein outside the weathered wooden livery stable. The building was tall, but looked as though it could fall over at any moment.

The gaunt figure dismounted in one slow fluid movement and looked at the livery stable carefully. There was evidence that the wooden planks had once been whitewashed. That had been a long time ago. Times were obviously tough in Silver Creek and folks never waste money on paint when they need to fill their bellies, he reasoned.

Iron Eyes held on to his reins tightly, then advanced into the dark void. He inhaled and could smell the horses at the far end of the livery. His head turned and he glanced at the forge with its red coals glowing in a mound beneath a crude but effective chimney.

'Anyone here?' he called out.

There was no answer but there came a noise of someone moving from an unseen room through the shadows towards him. The figure was rotund as all men of his profession were, but the flesh hid muscle. An awful lot of muscle. It took a lot of brawn to wrestle with a mustang that did not want to have shoes nailed to its hoofs.

Shafts of light from the walls' missing planks danced across the figure as he grunted towards the tall, emaciated figure and the palomino stallion.

Iron Eyes narrowed his eyes and focused on the man. He recognized him from all those years before because when it came to faces Iron Eyes never forgot one of them.

'Howdy, Bo,' Iron Eyes said in a rasping whisper.

The man stopped abruptly when he saw the face of his next customer. He rubbed the sweat off his brow and cleared his throat before managing to walk the last few yards to the strange figure. A figure he recognized.

Iron Eyes glared down at the shorter man. His bullet-coloured eyes reflected the fire of the forge behind the liveryman. It was like greeting the Devil.

'Howdy,' Bo Hartson managed to say.

'Ya got old,' the bounty hunter observed.

'Everybody does.'

'Unless ya kills 'em first.'

The liveryman regarded Iron Eyes up and down. Iron Eyes looked the same as he had all those years earlier, Hartson thought. Only the scars had increased across the emotionless face.

'That still your line of work, Iron Eyes? Killing folks, I mean.'

Iron Eyes nodded. 'Yep. I only kill those with paper on them though. Ain't no profit in just killing for the fun of it.'

Hartson exhaled loudly as though he had somehow managed to rein in his fear. He turned his attention to the stallion with its front left leg raised off the ground.

'Looks lame.'

'He is.'

'When did he go lame?' Hartson ran a massive hand down the horse's leg before lifting it so that he could see the damage more clearly in the sunlight.

'A few days back,' the bounty hunter answered as he strolled around inside the big building. 'He threw a shoe and then started to limp. Slowed me up a tad.'

'When did ya stop riding him?'

Iron Eyes looked at Hartson with a surprised expression on his mutilated features. 'Just now. I just got off him.'

'Ya mean that ya bin riding a lame horse until now?' the big man sounded and looked stunned by the admission. 'I never heard of such a thing. Ya could have crippled this fine animal for keeps.'

The bounty hunter pulled a long thin cigar from his deep bullet-filled trail-coat pocket, placed it between his teeth and moved towards the glowing coals.

'It's only a horse,' he said as he lifted a set of red-hot tongs and touched the tip of his cigar. He inhaled the smoke and then laid the irons down once more.

Hartson shook his head angrily. 'Ya still the same as ya always was. No thought for dumb critters. How can ya say that this handsome critter is only a horse?'

'Coz it is.' Iron Eyes blew out a line of smoke.

'Don't ya like him?'

'How can anyone like a damn horse?' The bounty hunter tilted his head and stared at the burly man as he began to remove the saddle and bags from the horse's back.

Hartson dumped the saddle at the feet of the thin tall man and made a strange noise through his nose. 'Ain't he got no value to you?'

'He is the fastest horse I've ever owned,' Iron Eyes admitted. He walked to the wide-open doors of the livery and looked out into the street. Apart from the movement of dust there was little to look at. 'He sure was slow after he threw that shoe though.'

'Ya could have crippled him.'

'Just put a shoe on him and I'll be on my way,' Iron Eyes said through a cloud of smoke. 'We got us a mighty slippery outlaw to catch up with.'

Bo Hartson moved right up to the bounty hunter and gritted his teeth. 'Ain't gonna get fixed by me nailing on a new shoe, Iron Eyes. This horse ain't going no place for a couple of weeks at the soonest.'

The expression on Iron Eyes's face changed as though some unseen fist had just smashed across his jaw. He took a step backwards, pulled the cigar from his teeth and pointed with it at the palomino.

'That just can't be,' he protested. 'I need him now. I gotta go up into the old country. I'm on the trail of a critter worth a thousand bucks or more. I can't sit in this town for weeks waiting for that nag. Just nail a new shoe on him. I'll pay top dollar.'

'Ya don't understand,' Hartson insisted. 'Ya done wrecked his leg. Every damn tendon is swollen and needs time and care to heal. That horse ain't leaving this stable 'til he's mended. Savvy?'

Iron Eyes stood like a statue, staring at the muscular blacksmith. For the first time since he had taken possession of the handsome stallion he showed a hint of concern for the animal.

'Will he be OK?'

'Yep.' Hartson gave a nod so forceful a shower of sweat splattered over the forge. It sounded like a dozen sidewinders as steam rose from the hot coals. 'But only if he rests the leg up for weeks.'

The bounty hunter rubbed his jaw. In the past he had never given a thought to the horse beneath him. Never even considered they deserved watering or being fed, but that had changed when he had killed the stallion's rider south of the border, only a year earlier. It had not taken long for Iron Eyes to realize that this was no Indian pony. No inbred mustang. This was a real horse. One which was strong and brave and capable of saving its master's life due to its turn of speed. Without even knowing it the bounty hunter had grown to rely upon the powerful animal and did not relish the idea of being without it.

'Listen up, Bo. I'll give ya four golden eagles to look after him,' Iron Eyes said. He pulled the coins from his coat pocket and stacked them on the top of an upturned barrel close to the forge. 'Ya make him better and I'll give ya the same again.'

Hartson was stunned. 'That's too much.'

'It's only money.' Iron Eyes looked the animal up and down and was confused by his own concern. He had shot more horses than he could remember over the years but he knew this horse deserved more than a seventeen-cent bullet between its ears. 'I might be gone for a few weeks or maybe more. Depends on how long it takes for me to get Two Fingers McGraw in my sights. The horse will be fixed by then. Right?'

The beefy man nodded. 'Reckon he'll be healed by then.'

'Good. Now sell me another horse.'

'Any particular kind of horse?'

Iron Eyes pulled a bottle of whiskey from his saddlebags and dragged its cork with his teeth. He spat the cork at the liveryman. 'Got any with four legs?'

Hartson led the stallion to a stall and

then stared at the gaunt, ghostlike creature before him. There was no understanding a man like Iron Eyes, he thought.

'When ya intend heading on out after this Two Fingers?'

Iron Eyes lowered the bottle from his scarred lips. 'As soon as ya gets my saddle on the back of a fresh nag, Bo.'

'What's the hurry?' the blacksmith opened the rear door of the building. A beam of morning sunlight flooded into the stables.

'Two Fingers must be getting a little long in the tooth by my reckoning.' Iron Eyes produced a Wanted poster from one of his pockets and waved it around as he followed the blacksmith into the heat of the corral. There were three horses roaming around that looked capable of finding pace should it be required. 'I gotta catch and kill the varmint before he up and dies of old age.'

Hartson levelled a long stare at the man who looked even worse in daylight than he did in shadows.

'Don't ya ever have no pity on the critters ya hunt?'

'Nope.' Iron Eyes pushed the well-worn poster back into his trail-coat pocket.

Hartson looked at the two gun grips which poked out from just above the pants they had been forced into. 'How come ya don't wear a gunbelt?'

'Ain't no call.' Iron Eyes shared the bottle with the blacksmith and pulled one of his guns. He spun it on his bony finger, then returned it into the gap where most men had flesh.

'Hold on a minute,' Hartson said, pointing at the pair of deadly Navy Colts. 'I thought them guns used ball and powder, not bullets.'

'Most do, but I had these altered by a mighty fine gunsmith in Laredo a long time ago.' The bounty hunter snatched his bottle back, poured the fiery liquid into his mouth and swallowed. 'Saves a whole heap of time, pushing bullets into chambers rather than messing with ball and powder. Used to take over five minutes to load these things before I had 'em converted.'

The blacksmith pointed at the strongest-looking of the horses. 'Will that'un do?'

Iron Eyes gave a silent nod.

'Ya said ya heading up to the old country?' Hartson said. He marched to the horse and grabbed its mane. He had begun to lead it towards the open doorway when the horse caught the scent of the bounty hunter. It shied. The aroma of death tended to linger on men like Iron Eyes.

'Yep. Had me some information that for some reason Two Fingers has been holed up in the forest.' Iron Eyes watched as Hartson led the animal into the shade to prepare it.

'Ain't like it was, boy,' Hartson said. He tossed a blanket on the back of the horse and patted it down. 'Half the forest bin cut down.'

'What for?'

'Lumber.'

17

Iron Eyes took another swig of the whiskey, then placed the bottle down next to the four golden coins. In all his days he had never managed to drink enough to make him drunk. He thought about the land where he had grown up. A land of trees and danger.

'That trouble ya?' Hartson hoisted the hefty Mexican saddle up on to the back of the nervous horse before reaching under its belly for the cinch straps. 'Folks cutting down all them trees?'

'Nope,' the bounty hunter answered as he plucked his saddle-bags up off the ground. 'Two Fingers will have less to hide behind if'n they've cut down half the trees. Might be useful if he's built like you, Bo.'

'I'm just solid muscle, boy.'

Iron Eyes glanced at the blacksmith. 'Got 'em well hid.'

The sound of barking suddenly filled the ears of both men. Without even thinking the bounty hunter drew and cocked one of his prized guns and swung round on his heels. The dog had caught the scent of death which hung on Iron Eyes. It was a smell no amount of scrubbing could ever vanquish and it alarmed most animals. The dog kept on barking as it drew nearer. Its teeth snapped at the tall man with the gun aimed at it.

'This your dog, Bo?'

'Nope.' Hartson had only just replied when Iron Eyes squeezed the trigger of his Navy Colt. A deafening flash spewed from its barrel. The dog yelped in pain and somersaulted. Covered in its own blood the dog fled, leaving its tail a few yards from the wide-open stable doors.

'I hates noisy dogs worse than I hates cowboys,' Iron Eyes muttered. He drew the spent casing from his gun and replaced it with a fresh bullet. He poked the gun down into his deep trail-coat pocket and gave a slight chuckle as he kicked the dog's tail aside. 'How ya gonna know when he's happy now, Bo?'

Stunned, Bo Hartson led the horse out into the sunlight and handed the reins to Iron Eyes.

'Ya headed out now, Iron Eyes?'

'After I stock up with provisions.' The bounty hunter tugged at the reins and began walking back along the main street, away from the livery stable.

Hartson scooped the four golden eagles off the barrel and then spotted the half-bottle of whiskey. Lifting up the bottle he glanced after Iron Eyes. The ghostlike figure was walking straight towards the saloon for his vital provisions.

The blacksmith took a swig and looked at the handsome palomino stallion before returning his attention to the man who owned it.

'How the devil did he ever get a horse like that?' As the whiskey trailed down his throat Hartson began to think he knew the answer.

1

The land grew more and more arid the further away from Silver Creek Iron Eyes rode the brown gelding. It seemed to Iron Eyes that the words of the blacksmith were true. The terrain had changed and not for the better. The once sheltered trail was now exposed to the elements. Dust and debris fell from the hoofs of the horse towards a swollen river that cut its way through the ancient territory far below. The rider's eyes narrowed as he drove his mount onward. He kept thinking of the outlaw he had followed to this place, and of the handsome bounty upon his head, yet something was screaming out to Iron Eyes to turn back. The further he rode the more the feeling grew.

It was as if he were riding towards his own demise, not that of the outlaw he sought. Iron Eyes drove on relentlessly even though he did not recognize half the land he was riding through. Now the quest was not just for Two Fingers McGraw but for the forest itself.

A forest that had vanished just as burly Bo Hartson had said it had. There was a disbelief in Iron Eyes as he surveyed the barren land that now surrounded him. The gelding moved nervously down into a dusty draw.

Iron Eyes drew rein and stopped the young mount. Blood dripped from his spurs as his thin form rose and balanced in his stirrups.

It looked so different from the way it had done all those years before, when he had last ridden this trail upon a stolen Indian pony. Nothing was recognizable.

The draw had once been filled with countless trees feeding off a narrow stream, but now, without the trees, the water was gone. Only dust remained.

Iron Eyes lowered himself in to the saddle again and rubbed his jaw thoughtfully. There was no trace of the men who had cut down this section of the once dense forest. They had moved on to far greener pastures.

The thin rider dismounted and held on to the long leathers until he found something he could secure them to. He knew this new mount would take flight given half a chance.

The skeletal figure moved around the dusty draw as though searching, not for the outlaw who had brought him back to this place, but for something which he might easily recognize.

Long ago he had been able to travel through the forest and never lose his bearings even if he were blindfolded. Now, with his eyes wide open, Iron Eyes doubted everything around him.

Where was he?

Iron Eyes spat at the ground and kicked at the dust.

Hartson had been right.

This place was no longer the same.

It looked more like a battlefield than the once fertile forest where he had matured into adulthood and honed his skills as a hunter. For half his life he had moved around this forest unseen by those who grew to fear him. He had used its every tree and bush to conceal himself until the Indians had started to believe him to be a ghost.

A deadly phantom.

Now it was all gone.

It existed only in his mind.

A forest had become little more than a memory.

The horse never took its eyes from the man who walked silently around the draw. It snorted and vainly pulled at its leathers but there was no escape. Like the countless horses that had gone before it, the animal was at the mercy of a man who had little liking for the creatures he rode.

Iron Eyes strode back to the gelding, tore the reins free and then mounted swiftly. He was unhappy and he did not understand why.

He gathered in his reins and rested a hand on top of his saddle horn. Once more he looked around the area for something that had not been destroyed by the axes and saws of those who had virtually stripped it clean of trees. He had thought that when he followed Two Fingers McGraw into this forest he would easily be able to hunt him down; the outlaw would not stand a chance against his superior knowledge of the forest. Now Iron Eyes doubted that he might be able even to pick up Two Fingers's trail, let alone trap and kill him.

His bullet-coloured eyes narrowed.

A heat haze shimmered in the air before him, masking anything further than a quarter-mile from where his horse stood. Iron Eyes knew he had to move to higher ground if he were to find a familiar landmark.

The horseman tapped his spurs again into the already bloody flesh of his mount. The gelding raced along the draw. A thousand thoughts filled the mind of the bounty hunter.

None of them concerned the outlaw he was meant to be hunting.

For another three miles Iron Eyes rode through the draw and noticed nothing alive apart from the occasional tree, which had somehow managed to survive the saws and axes of those who had stripped the area clean.

A plague of locusts could not have done a better job.

There was a vast forest ahead, Iron Eyes told himself. Or at least there used to be. He drove his spurs deep into the flanks of the horse and charged up a slope until he was atop a dusty crest.

He screwed up his eyes against the noisome heat haze and stared in disbelief at the sun-baked ground that rolled on ahead of him. The once dark-green forest of trees had been replaced by tree stumps. Stumps which looked like tombstones to his tired eyes. In a way that was what they were. They were the tombstones of a forest.

Iron Eyes pulled out a cigar, rammed it between his teeth and snorted angrily. He struck the match with his thumb-nail, sucked in its flame as smoke filled his lungs. He kept staring in disbelief at the rolling hills before him.

It was dead.

Only where the hills reached the mountainous slopes did the tree line remain. They had not been felled yet but it was only a matter of time, he told himself.

He glanced to both sides. Far to his left there were more trees and signs of life. Smoke from a campfire spiralled up into the blue sky. That must be where the lumberjacks had their camp, Iron Eyes mused.

The land before him had been cleared by a team of men who knew their job. Iron Eyes could see sunlight dancing upon a wide river about two miles from where he rested. Even from the distance between the bounty hunter and the river he could still make out that it was full of trimmed trees.

He sucked in the smoke even deeper.

The stiff breeze which once could not have penetrated the forest now had nothing to prevent it from destroying what was left of the once magnificent land before him. With every passing second more of the once rich topsoil was blown away.

'Them lumberjacks sure done a good job of clearing this place of timber, horse,' Iron Eyes rasped.

He thought about the outlaw who, he had been told, was hiding out in this forest. How could he find Two Fingers when he could not even find the forest?

It seemed to Iron Eyes that no one in his right mind would choose to hide here. You needed brush and cover to hide and that was in short supply wherever he cast his determined gaze.

Iron Eyes was about to spur on when he saw something that he had not expected. Something that made him ease himself off the back of his horse and walk towards it.

The bounty hunter stood holding the reins in one hand and his cigar in the other. The dusty surface of the ground was moving like a sidewinder as the breeze continued to blow across its fragile surface. He stepped closer to the barely visible object poking out of the sand.

Iron Eyes kicked at it with his mule-eared boot, then lowered his head until his mane of black hair fell over his hideous features.

Suddenly it was clear what it was at his feet.

He returned the cigar to his teeth and chewed on it as his eyes focused hard.

It was a man's hand.

2

Iron Eyes knelt and brushed at the dust. The flesh had dried and turned to something frail like dried paper. The more dust he removed from the body the clearer it became to his honed eyesight that this was the remains of a white man in a shallow grave. The boots were not that of a cowboy or a drifting rider's but more akin to the sort worn by the men who felled trees. They were laced and sturdy with metal toecaps.

'Lumberjack,' the bounty hunter said through a cloud of smoke as the cigar nestled in the corner of his scarred mouth.

He continued to brush the dust off the torso of the corpse; then he felt something familiar against his finger-tips.

It was an arrow.

An arrow poked out from the centre

of the dead man's chest. Iron Eyes tugged the arrow free, stood up and then studied the deadly projectile. Then he turned his head to look at the skittish horse.

'Hell. I'd plumb forgot about them damn Injuns in the forest, horse,' he muttered. He grabbed his saddle horn, poked his pointed boot-toe into his stirrup and hoisted himself aloft.

Iron Eyes sat and blew the dust off the arrow's feathered flights. His keen eyes studied the object in his hands for a few moments, then he slid it into his rifle scabbard until only its feathers could be seen.

'I sure hope them Injuns ain't still around,' Iron Eyes muttered as he reached back and lifted out one of the bottles from his saddle-bags. He pulled its cork and spat it away. 'I sure ain't hankering to tangle with them again.'

The bounty hunter lifted the bottle and drank what remained of the whiskey in three long swallows. He then tossed the bottle aside. The horse flinched as the glass shattered.

Iron Eyes dried his mouth along his coat sleeve and then, for some reason, looked down at the arrow's flights once more. His bony fingers pulled the arrow free again and he studied the feathers closely.

Something was wrong.

He knew the colours of the feathers that the forest's braves always used on their arrows. This flight was different. The bounty hunter was puzzled.

'There must be another tribe in the forest. One that I never met up with before.' Iron Eyes threw the arrow over his bony shoulder.

He knew he had to get to the trees far ahead of him.

He spurred hard.

His horse thundered on.

3

A dustcloud rose from the hoofs of the gelding as it galloped across the wide expanse of arid terrain in search of the forest that Iron Eyes knew would protect him, as it had always done. Yet for the first time since he had started hunting men Iron Eyes doubted the wisdom of this particular hunt.

He sensed danger all around him here. It was as though the very air itself was warning him to quit, but that was not his way.

He drew rein and watched the dust continue to rise.

The skeletal figure drove his right hand deep into the trail-coat pocket. Iron Eyes withdrew the folded Wanted poster. It was weathered and brown. Like the man he was hunting it had probably seen better days. He unfolded the paper and stared at the crude image on it.

The face could have fitted a hundred of the outlaws whom Iron Eyes had hunted over the previous few years, but it was the wording that gave the clue as to how he could identify Two Fingers McGraw.

'Has an inch-long scar on his chin running down his throat,' Iron Eyes read aloud. 'Has first two fingers missing from his left hand. Ain't you the pretty boy?'

He rubbed a finger across the $1,000 price on the paper and nodded to himself. He knew that by now that sum must have increased.

A satisfied grin found the cruel scars of the bounty hunter as he carefully folded the paper up and returned it to the deep coat pocket.

'Reckon I oughta be able to pick that varmint out of a crowd of chicken pluckers, horse.' He smirked.

Iron Eyes looked around him. Then his bullet-coloured eyes focused beyond the heat haze and the desolation. A crooked smile covered his face. The major part of the forest was still there. It rose up the sides of the mountains.

He knew that his prey must be there.

That was where he would find McGraw.

Iron Eyes toyed with the reins in his left hand. 'I'll find you, Two Fingers. Find and kill you. Wanted dead or alive means dead in my book. There ain't no other way.'

The thin figure rose off his saddle, balanced in his stirrups and whipped the long leathers across his mount's tail. The horse responded and started to trot.

'C'mon, horse.'

The horse gained pace as its long legs ate up the dry ground beneath its hoofs.

The bounty hunter sat down just as the sound of gunfire suddenly filled the air off to his right. Iron Eyes swung the gelding around and squinted into the sun, to where he had heard the noise of shooting. Then another noise piqued his interest. That of yelling men.

At first the rider thought it was the war cries of the Indians who, he knew, had once existed in the forest, but then he started to doubt his ears. There was something different about the excited calls. Something which confused Iron Eyes.

Rifle shots rang out.

Then more excited ranting.

The chilling memory of the forest's children swept over the bounty hunter. He had heard their battle calls many times during his youth.

The shooting grew even more intense.

There were Indians out there, he told himself. They had locked horns with somebody they regarded as an enemy. To Iron Eyes that meant lumberjacks. He knew the sort of men who risked their lives cutting down entire forests. They respected no laws of any kind. They were a breed apart and did not allow anyone to stop them from earning a living.

The gelding was terrified. It took

every ounce of his strength for the bounty hunter to hold the animal in check.

The shooting and raised voices increased in volume.

Iron Eyes could see gunsmoke rising from somewhere just beyond the trees to his right. An awful lot of gunsmoke.

The deafening shooting became frantic, the war cries even more urgent. Iron Eyes looked straight ahead at the line of dark trees and knew there was sanctuary there. Yet the battle was an equal distance from the lone horseman.

Iron Eyes had tangled with many tribes over the years, but the most dangerous were those with whom he had shared the forest. His mind flashed back to the arrow he had found in the dead man a few miles back.

Were these the same warriors? Or perhaps an even more fearsome tribe. Either way he did not want to find out.

Then, as quickly as the shooting had begun, it stopped.

Iron Eyes instinctively knew who had

won that short battle and it was not the lumberjacks.

His mind raced. Could he make it to the forest? There was no cover and that was not good. There was only one way to find out though. He drove his spurs deep into the flesh of his horse.

'C'mon, horse!' he yelled.

The animal obeyed its master and thundered towards the tree line, which was still a couple of miles ahead. The brown gelding reached a pace it had not managed to attain before.

Yet even at full speed Iron Eyes realized that this was just a saddle horse like so many other saddle horses. There was no way it could equal the pace of the palomino stallion he had left with Bo Hartson. It had no fire in its belly. No spirit in its pounding heart. All it had was the fear of the relentless spurs.

Leaning as far over the neck of the horse as he dared, Iron Eyes tried to take the weight off its shoulders. Yet even that made no difference. The horse was slowing even though it was trying to escape the spurs of its master.

Ahead of him through the heat haze Iron Eyes could just make out a line of painted ponies.

They were between him and his goal.

The bounty hunter dragged his reins up to his chest just as a flash of a rifle caught his eye. The shot had been fired from the middle of the line of horsemen. The slowing horse buckled beneath Iron Eyes.

The animal hit the ground hard and rolled over the bounty hunter before coming to a rest on its belly beside him.

Iron Eyes somehow scrambled back to his feet. Then another bullet flew past the scarecrow figure before a third lifted the tails of his long trail coat up and almost dragged him off his feet.

The dazed bounty hunter scooped up his guns off the sand and dropped them into his deep coat pockets. He could hear more shots being fired. Luckily every bullet failed to find their target. Only men who were as painfully thin as Iron Eyes could have escaped the deadly lead.

The bony hands of the stunned man grabbed the reins of the horse, which was still on its belly. He knew the animal had been hit by a bullet and that was why it had fallen so violently, but there was no time for concern. No time for pity. Only time to try and survive.

Iron Eyes saw the blood that covered its chest as he feverishly urged the horse to rise. He tugged at the reins over and over again.

'Ya better get up, horse,' Iron Eyes yelled at the wounded animal. 'If ya don't them varmints will come on over here and kill me and probably eat you. Get the hell up.'

As more shots kicked up the ground around him the horse somehow managed to get back to its feet. It wavered like a newly born foal. It was shaking as it stood beside him. Iron Eyes gave the weeping bullet hole another glance, then grabbed the loose reins, poked a boot-toe into the stirrup and mounted.

'You gonna ride, horse?' Iron Eyes

felt his long hair move as a bullet cut across his cheek and carved a deep gash into his already mutilated flesh. He screamed in agony and shook a fist at the heavens. 'Damn it all. I ain't bin cutting down no trees.'

Even a lifetime of battles had not prepared him for this unexpected turn of events. The hunter was now the hunted. He was the target and he would be mighty lucky to survive.

There was no time to consider how badly wounded the gelding was. Iron Eyes was now pumping blood himself. A lot of blood. He swung the horse's head round to where he had heard the gunfight, then rammed both his spurs back.

The horse responded and started to find pace.

Now both man and beast were losing blood with each beat of their hearts. A blind man could have followed the crimson trail they were leaving in their wake. The animal kept on obeying the spurs as its master hung over its neck and tried to see the men who were firing the rifles behind them.

Dust rose above the line of horsemen and Iron Eyes realized that they were now in pursuit.

'Keep going,' the bounty hunter snarled at his horse as he saw the line of trees he was aiming at getting closer. He turned again and suddenly heard the war cries sounding behind him. They were gaining on him.

As he came closer to where the brief battle had occurred he saw the bodies of the lumberjacks. They were strewn all around the makeshift campsite.

The aroma of gunsmoke filled his flared nostrils. The camp was on a slope and he could feel his wounded horse labouring as it tried to ascend the steep rise.

A handful of trees left as a windbreak masked a couple of wagons beyond. Smoke billowed from a campfire set in the centre of the site. Once-stalwart men lay dead everywhere; their sinewy muscles had proved impotent against the arrows and bullets that had ended their existence.

Iron Eyes knew their breed only too well.

They did as their distant paymasters ordered.

Their only law was gun law. To the bounty hunter they deserved all they got but that did not stop the wailing of the riders behind him. Iron Eyes swung around and half-closed his eyes. He could see the painted faces getting closer.

Iron Eyes spurred the half-dead gelding. It managed to reach a huge wagon perched on the edge of the slope before it stopped and fell to its knees.

It was finished and its new master knew it. The bounty hunter looped his right leg over the animal's neck and looked back at the Indians. Bullets and arrows flew past him and became embedded in the wagons side.

Iron Eyes had to do something and fast, he told himself.

But what? He gave the charging

warriors a glance full of hatred and ran to the wagon's tailgate. It was lowered, revealing what lay on the flatbed. Boxes of dynamite and coils of fuse wire filled the vehicle's canvassed interior.

'That's it!' Iron Eyes said. He dragged out a length of fuse wire and rammed it into one of the dynamite sticks. He cut the fuse short, then plucked the smouldering cigar from his lips.

He rubbed blood from his face along his sleeve and touched the end of the fuse with the glowing tip of his cigar.

A sound like a sidewinder filled his ears as the sparks began to spit from the quickly vanishing wire.

There was no way of knowing how long the fuse would take to reach the explosives, making them erupt into unimaginable fury. Iron Eyes threw the cigar aside and ran to the front of the wagon. He released the brake pole and shouldered the hefty wheel until it started to move.

Gravity did its job well. The heavily

laden vehicle moved over the rim of the slope and gained momentum. It rolled down to where the Indians were. The riders had to scatter as the massive wagon weaved its way between the nine horsemen.

Only one of the horsemen continued on towards Iron Eyes.

The bounty hunter pulled both his Navy Colts free and cocked their hammers.

He was ready to fight.

He was ready to die.

His eyes narrowed as he saw the rifle in the rider's hands being cocked and levelled at him. There was no place to hide, Iron Eyes told himself. He raised and aimed his weaponry.

His fingers had no sooner squeezed the triggers than the wagon blew up in a myriad glowing fragments. The entire area rocked as more and more of the dynamite sticks exploded. Fiery shards of debris flew in all directions as curling black smoke went heavenward.

The rider had not had time to fire his

rifle before both of the bounty hunter's bullets tore through his chest. The Indian crashed into the dust at Iron Eyes's feet, still clutching his Winchester in his hands.

Iron Eyes dropped both his guns into his deep coat pockets and stepped over the body. He grabbed the reins of the pony and led it to where his dead gelding lay in a pool of its own blood.

His bony hands secured the reins to the saddle horn of the fallen mount.

Iron Eyes hated killing Indians.

There was no profit in it.

4

The fearsome black smoke engulfed the
entire hillside, filling the bounty hunter's flared nostrils with its acrid stench.
The ground itself was rocking beneath
the bounty hunter's boots as one
explosion followed another. A million
fiery splinters blew away from where
the wagon had been only seconds
earlier. Now there was only a crater: a
smouldering crater. Iron Eyes moved
quickly to the line of trees and rested a
shoulder against the broadest of them.
Blood kept pumping from the hideous
wound on his cheek as he studied the
death and mayhem he had just created.

There was not one hint of any
emotion in the long, thin, skeletal
figure. Only relief that it had been they
who had died and not him.

'That'll learn ya.' Iron Eyes spat in
the direction of the deep hole in the

ground. It smouldered as the flames fed off wood and bodies alike. 'Tangle with me and you end up dead.'

The air was thick with the foul smoke. Smoke which was unlike any he had ever experienced before. It contained the dust not only of the wagon but of men and beasts in its choking vapour.

This was not just killing, Iron Eyes thought, this was wholesale slaughter. He had killed many men before with bullets and the honed edge of his Bowie knife, but he had never killed like this.

Not with dynamite.

He did not like it.

From head to toe he was being coated in the sickening filth of his victory. Iron Eyes took no pleasure from it.

His eyes searched for his victims' bodies.

The blood flowed from the deep gash across his face as he turned back towards the campsite. He stared at the large fire at its centre and paced towards it.

With every step the haunting jingle of his sharp spurs rang out. When he reached the fire he leaned down and pulled his long Bowie knife from the neck of his right boot. Its blade flashed in the bright afternoon sunlight. Iron Eyes knelt and poked the blade into the hottest-looking part of the fire and held on to its handle. He turned the knife over as if it wcrc a spit holding a pig until he knew the metal blade had absorbed heat from the fire.

Over the years the fearless bounty hunter had been forced to stem the flow of blood from many horrific injuries on his emaciated body by searing his skin with a hot iron. He gritted his teeth, then swiftly raised the knife and pressed its red-hot blade against his bleeding flesh.

It sounded like bacon in a skillet. It hissed like a rattler as he moved the hot edge over the wound.

Defying the agony of sizzling flesh

Iron Eyes kept the hot steel pressed against his face until he was sure he had managed to stem the bleeding and seal the torn flesh together.

It seemed like an eternity.

Iron Eyes then dropped the knife. He doubled up in silent torment. He rocked on his knees but refused to scream out in pain even though the only people who might have heard were already dead.

He chewed on the pain.

He swallowed it whole and knew it had not defeated him. Pain could be handled if you refused to acknowledge it. That was what he always told himself even though, deep down in his guts, he did not believe it.

Iron Eyes looked at the campfire through the limp strands of his matted black hair. He stared into the fire and watched the flames dancing hypnotically before him. Slowly he managed to summon the strength he required to continue. He snatched the knife off the sand and rose to his full height. Most men would have needed more time to recover, but not Iron Eyes.

He touched the raw burned flesh on his face and snorted. Yet more scars to add to those that already covered his face and body, he thought.

Iron Eyes looked at the knife and rubbed it across his coat sleeve. He slid the long-bladed weapon back into the neck of his boot and turned.

He studied carefully the scene of death and destruction that surrounded him. It did not take long for the bounty hunter to walk around the area and check the faces of the dead men. So many dead men and not a wanted man amongst them.

'This is turning out to be a mighty expensive day,' Iron Eyes complained to himself.

His attention returned to that of the dead horse and the Indian horse that he had tethered to its saddle horn. He walked back to the body of his dead horse and stared angrily at it.

'Ya might have turned out to be a

good nag if you hadn't let yourself get shot.' Iron Eyes kicked the flap of one of the saddle-bag satchels open. He stooped, grabbed a full bottle of whiskey and straightened up once more. He tore its cork from the glass neck and spat it away. He poured some of the whiskey over the red-raw wound on his face and winced.

Then he sucked on the bottle neck and savoured every drop of the amber liquid as the whiskey burned its way down into his belly. He only lowered the bottle when he needed air in his lungs.

His cold bullet-coloured eyes stared out at the slope again, at the smoke that still rose from the the burned ground. Every one of the Indian warriors who had been close to the wagon when it exploded was gone. Even their horses had vanished.

Iron Eyes downed more of the whiskey. They had been after his scalp and somehow he had managed to get the better of them.

He glanced back at his dead mount, then looked at the painted pony tethered to his ornate Mexican saddle. He was about to take another swig from the bottle when something unexpected caught his attention.

The bounty hunter moved closer to the terrified horse and looked at its bridle.

It was leather.

Iron Eyes slid the bottle into one of his deep coat pockets, took hold of the bridle and pulled the head of the horse towards him. His eyes studied the bridle.

It was of leather and metal. There was even a bit in the horse's mouth. The sort of bit that Bo Hartson fashioned on his forge back at Silver Creek.

In all his days Iron Eyes had never known any Indian of any tribe to use a metal bit to control his mount. Indians tended to use a rope, which was looped around the head and jaw of the animal they rode.

'This is a white man's bridle!' Iron

Eyes exclaimed in total surprise. 'Damned if that ain't mighty curious.'

Then he saw something else which drew his gaze along the body of the frightened pony. Beneath the blanket on the animal's back there was a hidden saddle. A Texas saddle with two cinch straps.

Iron Eyes tore the blanket free and dropped it on to the ground. His mind raced in search of explanation.

'This Injun could have killed a white *hombre* and just stole his saddle and gear, I guess,' the thin man conjectured. 'I never known any of them to do that though. They usually only need themselves a blanket. Why'd this'un want a damn saddle and a bridle? It don't figure.'

Another thought came to the bounty hunter. He ran a bony hand down the leg of the skittish animal, grabbed at the leg and lifted it off the ground. It was shod. No Indian pony was ever shod with the metal horseshoes white men favoured.

Confused, Iron Eyes walked to where the body of the brave lay in a pool of its own gore.

'You came real close to killing me,' the bounty hunter said with a sigh. 'But you made me waste two bullets. There sure ain't no profit in killing critters without bounty on their heads.'

Iron Eyes shook his head and stared back at the horse that was not what it feigned to be. He leaned down and grabbed the Indian's mane of black hair and was about to turn the body over when the hair came away in his hand.

For a moment Iron Eyes was startled. He stared at the black wig in his hand and then down at the body on the ground. The body of a bald man.

'What in tarnation is going on here?' Iron Eyes dropped on to one knee and turned the body over. He stared at the painted face. Then he rubbed at the face with the wig in his hand. At first the paint came off on to the wig, then the underlay of colouring that had made the white man appear far darker than he truly was. 'Damn. This critter is covered with grease. Grease with colour in it.'

Iron Eyes rose back up and tossed the hairpiece aside.

'If this'un was a white man then they must have all bin white men,' he told himself as his thin fingers retrieved his whiskey bottle from his pocket. 'White men disguised as red men to attack other white men. Why'd they want to do that? Why'd they want Injuns to get the blame?'

The answer came just as the last droplet of whiskey trailed down his throat. He tossed the bottle over his shoulder and nodded to himself.

'It must be all the timber these lumberjacks have cut down and have fenced off down in the river,' Iron Eyes said, looking at the bodies scattered all about him. 'Yep. That's it. Some smart bunch of varmints let these critters do all the hard work and now they've decided to steal it.'

Iron Eyes was impressed.

He pulled a twisted cigar from his pocket, straightened it and rammed it into his mouth. He was about to strike a match when something high amid the trees caught his attention. He stepped forward and narrowed his gaze.

Something was catching the rays of the sun.

What was it? Iron Eyes knew it could be one of many things. It might be the polished magazine of a carbine. It might be a bottle, like the one he had just thrown away. It could also be a belt buckle or even the polished tip of an Indian lance.

It could be any thing, none of which was natural.

No animal or anything else he knew of in nature reflected the rays of the sun like that. Whatever it was, it belonged to a man. A man who had probably been drawn to the noise of the gunfight or the deafening explosion that had followed.

Iron Eyes knew that someone up on the tree-covered hillside was now watching the only survivor of the outrage. Watching from a high vantage point that gave him an advantage. Whoever it was, he could pick Iron Eyes off easily.

Could it be Two Fingers McGraw?

Maybe it was real Indians.

Whoever it was Iron Eyes knew that he held all the aces. It would be easy for anyone with a rifle to shoot him whilst he stood amid the carnage of the campsite.

The bounty hunter found a match in his shirt pocket while he kept looking up into the dense forested hillside that loomed above.

Iron Eyes knew that whoever was up there was far beyond the range of his trusty Navy Colts. He moved like a panther across the clearing towards the painted pony tied to his own dead mount. He scratched his thumbnail across the top of the match and cupped its flame to the cigar gripped between his teeth. He inhaled the putrid smoke but never took his eyes from the flashing of the unknown object as it moved slowly between the trees. With every beat of his heart Iron Eyes knew the sun was slowly sinking towards the land behind him. Soon the brilliant rays would not shed light upon the man high above him. Soon the bounty hunter would have no idea where the man was.

Then suddenly he heard something. It was the sound of pounding horses' hoofs heading towards him. His eyes screwed up and stared out across the barren landscape below the screen of trees, searching for the riders.

All he could see was dust rising. A lot of dust.

'That sure ain't good.' Iron Eyes exhaled a long grey line of smoke at the ground. 'Reckon I got company coming. I'll wager they got something to do with either these lumberjacks or them phoney Injuns. Either way I'm going to get the blame for all these damn dead bodies.'

Iron Eyes spun on his heels.

He realized time was short. There was urgency in his movements as he knelt in the blood of his dead horse, undid the cinch straps and grabbed the hefty Mexican saddle. He pulled it free of the lifeless animal's carcass.

The skeletal figure staggered to the painted pony and dropped his burden at its front hoofs. It did not take long for his bony hands to remove the saddle from the back of the skittish painted pony and replace it with his own far heavier one. Iron Eyes hastily buckled the cinch straps of the saddle which had once belonged to a Mexican *vaquero*. He then threw the saddle-bags up behind the saddle cantle and secured them.

The bounty hunter looped the reins over the head and neck of the horse, then quickly stepped into his stirrup. He hoisted himself aloft and held the nervous horse in check.

Iron Eyes expertly controlled the animal beneath him as he listened to the sound of hoofbeats as the oncomers pounded to close the distance between themselves and the camp.

The infamous horseman pulled the spent cigar from his teeth, tossed it at the blood-soaked ground and spat. His eyes returned to the dense screen of trees.

Then he saw it.

A clear gap between the trees.

Then he saw something else.

For the first time since he had returned to his old hunting grounds Iron Eyes actually recognized a natural feature. A massive oak tree stood next to the gap in the screen of entangled branches and undergrowth. Not just any oak tree but one he knew like an old friend.

This was the very same oak tree he knew from his days as a boy and youth. It was the one constant in an ever changing forest: it had never let Iron Eyes down. It had sheltered and protected him from the elements as well as the deadly creatures that roamed the once limitless tract of trees.

Iron Eyes remembered that there was a strange scarred shape on its trunk. The only reminder of a branch that had been broken from the great oak many years ago. Over the years, the shape had turned into something which looked like a human face.

The sound of the riders caught the horseman's ears again. They were now really close, he told himself. Iron Eyes slapped his reins and spurred the painted pony into action. The terrified animal raced across the clearing towards the great oak and the trail that lay beside it.

'C'mon, horse,' Iron Eyes yelled into the ear of the animal beneath him.

With each stride of the pony the rider knew he was right. It was the very same tree. The last time he had seen that tree it had been deep in the heart of the forest. Now it was on the very edge of what remained of the once vast expanse of trees.

He stared ahead as his hands worked the long reins. The massive branches spread out from the wide trunk like the arms of a monster. The closer Iron Eyes got to the tree and the darkness of the ancient woodland, the more he could smell the scent of his old home.

'C'mon, horse. We ain't got much time,' Iron Eyes raged as he kept thrashing the long leathers across the shoulders of his new mount. He glanced to his side. The dust from the approaching riders' horses hoofs was mixing with the smoke from the burning debris on the slope.

There remained only twenty yards to where the time-scarred oak tree stood and the painted horse was gaining pace with every long stride.

It was dark inside the forest.

Yet he knew there was safety in the ancient shadows.

Iron Eyes recalled that several trails led in all directions beyond the oak tree and he knew them all. They were branded into his memory. All he had to do was reach the darkness where the scent of centuries lingered and he would be safe.

Suddenly a shot rang out.

A deadly flash of smouldering lead cut across the path of the bounty hunter's horse but Iron Eyes' driving spurs kept the terrified animal moving. Then more shots followed until the sound was deafening. The air stank with gunsmoke as bullets tore all around him in search of his emaciated frame.

It was as though a hive of crazed hornets had suddenly attacked him. He felt his long coat tails being torn from behind his legs as he balanced in his stirrups.

More shots rained in upon him.

One hit the well-padded cantle and sent the thundering pony staggering to its right as another hit the left satchel of his bags. The sound of whiskey bottles smashing was mixed with the pungent vapours of the hard liquor, which swirled around both horse and master.

The bounty hunter clawed one of his Navy Colts from his pocket, cocked and fired back at the thundering horsemen who were gaining on him. Yet more bullets caught the heavy saddle and sent the terrified horse careering off course. Iron Eyes swung the animal around and furiously fanned his gun hammer.

When the long-barrelled weapon was empty Iron Eyes rammed it back into his pocket and whipped the shoulders of his horse once more. The animal responded and raced into the darkness of the forest beyond the great oak tree.

No sooner had the painted pony cleared the sun-baked ground than the trunk of the large tree exploded: a fusillade of bullets hit it. Bark was turned into a million splinters. The smell of burning wood followed the rider into the shadowy interior of the forest.

'Damn it all!' Iron Eyes raged. He hauled rein and spun the horse round to face the brightly lit land he had just managed to flee. He rose and balanced in his stirrups. 'I'm starting to get mighty tired of folks shooting at me.'

He stared through the leafy branches at the dozen or more riders who galloped past the well-concealed gap in the tangle of branches and undergrowth. It soon dawned on Iron Eyes that, just like him, the mounted gunmen had not been able to see their target clearly. They had not seen him escape their venom into the forest.

Iron Eyes speedily checked himself. He had not been hit this time, unlike earlier. Only the tails of his long trail coat showed the damage caused by the bullets. They were shredded as though they had been attacked by something like a puma.

Iron Eyes leaned over the neck of his panting mount and peered out into the bright land as clouds of hoof dust hung on the dry air. It was in total contrast to the cool of the shaded place he rested in. The choking dust of the riders had disguised the route he had taken to escape their deadly lead.

But the bounty hunter had a feeling

that it would not be long before these men found his trail. Only the setting of the sun could delay their chase, he told himself. Iron Eyes squinted across the vast terrain which faced him. He calculated that the sun would be setting in roughly an hour.

Would it be enough time for his hoof tracks to be hidden from the riders? Darkness could not arrive soon enough. The horse snorted as it was dragged mercilessly around to face the eerie half-light of the forest interior.

Iron Eyes looked all around him.

He had no idea where he was going but knew that it would pay to find higher ground. He spotted a familiar trail that seemed not to have altered in all the years since he had last seen it.

That was the trail he had to take.

The narrow clay pathway led to higher land and a place where he could defend himself from an entire army.

He was about to spur when he caught the scent of whiskey in his flared nostrils. Then he recalled the bullets which had hit the saddle-bag where he kept half of his liquid provisions. Iron Eyes twisted and leaned back. His bony fingers opened the bullet-ridden satchel of his bags. Three bottles of whiskey had been shattered inside the bag.

Desperately Iron Eyes checked the other bag. To his relief the four bottles inside that satchel were intact. He returned his fingers to the bullet-ridden satchel and carefully lifted up the bottom half of one of the broken bottles.

The bounty hunter straightened up and looked at the amber contents of the whiskey bottle. Then, ignoring the jagged edges of the bottle, he lifted it to his scarred lips. He carefully filled his mouth with the whiskey and swilled it around his tongue and teeth. He swallowed and gave a shudder.

'Damned if it don't taste better with glass in it.' He coughed and filled his mouth again. This time as he washed the whiskey around his tongue he felt something touching his teeth. He tentatively plucked the small lump of lead from his lips and swallowed again. He stared at what was left of the bullet, then threw it and the broken bottle down upon the ground angrily.

He was about to curse when he heard the muffled voices of the horsemen out near the campsite. Leaning close to the oak tree the curious bounty hunter squinted through the undergrowth at the horsemen who had reached the campsite.

They were not dressed like Indians. They were not even dressed like lumberjacks. The dozen or so riders were dressed like cowboys. Yet the bounty hunter felt that these men were something far more dangerous than mere cowboys.

The sunlight danced off their weaponry, some holstered, the rest held in their gloved hands. Each rider had more than enough weapons hanging not only from his gunbelt but his saddle as well. They were loaded for bear and Iron Eyes knew that he was the bear.

Iron Eyes spat. These gunmen were dangerous. They were hired gunslingers and that was the worst breed of men he had ever encountered over the years. Money was all they thought about and they would kill anyone if the price was right. They had no loyalty to anything except their evil paymasters' swollen wallets. Their paymasters paid well for them to do their killing for them, so that their own hands were never soiled.

'That's mighty curious and a tad troubling,' Iron Eyes whispered before he straightened up and turned his mount back to where the trail to higher ground started. A thought dawned on him. 'Hell. I've ridden into some kinda war here and whoever them varmints are, they figure I'm on their enemy's side. No wonder they was shooting at me.'

Thoughtfully Iron Eyes placed a cigar between his teeth and started to chew on it.

He spurred.

5

The afternoon sun was low sinking beyond the tree-fringed hillside to the west of the settlement. The blue sky which stretched across the heavens above Silver Creek had begun to take on the colour of the fire in the livery stable's forge. It was as though the very clouds had suddenly erupted into flame. To those who still remained within the confines of the town it was a chilling sight that usually heralded misfortune or even worse.

As the sky grew redder their fears appeared to have some basis in fact. For as the shadows became blacker and longer and everything seemed to be bathed in a scarlet hue, an unfamiliar sound filled the streets. It was the sound of thundering hoofs and rattling chains. Then the cracking of a whip also joined in the unholy crescendo.

Men and women raised hands to shield their eyes against the almost blinding rays of the low sun. They were afraid but wanted to see what it was that was coming towards their remote and almost abandoned community. Whatever it was it was not welcomed by the people who had resigned themselves to living their final days unhindered by those from the outside world.

A world that had turned its back on them years earlier when the precious ore had run out.

The black silhouette of the approaching vehicle with the dying embers of a fiery sun behind it did nothing to ease the concerns of the town's onlookers. What they saw was in itself something that confused and frightened every last one of them.

It was like casting one's eyes upon the Devil himself atop a fiery chariot. The people fled in terror to their homes. Even those who had been in the saloon before their curiosity had been whetted by the noise turned on their heels and ran as though they had witnessed something straight from the bowels of Hell.

At the other end of Silver Creek, in the livery stable the brawny blacksmith was entirely unaware of the alarm his fellow townsfolk were experiencing on the arrival of yet another unexpected visitor to their secluded settlement.

Bo Hartson had been working hard on the lame stallion left in his care by Iron Eyes. There were few things he did not know when it came to tending horses. During the hours since the bounty hunter had ridden out from Silver Creek the liveryman had massaged liniment into the weary animal's injured leg and had managed to bind it from hoof to shoulder. Now recovery would need rest for the palomino stallion; Hartson was determined the animal would get plenty of that.

Hartson had only just screwed the top back on the liniment bottle and was about to place it back on the wooden shelf next to the forge when he heard raised voices out in the street.

They were panicking again, the large man told himself as he ran the palms of both hands down his apron.

Panicking just like they had when they had set eyes upon the haunting figure of Iron Eyes hours earlier.

Hartson had the palomino tied securely to one of the many supporting timbers that stretched from the ground up to the hay loft. He patted the horse, then ambled towards the wide-open doors and the street bathed in the crimson hues of sunset.

'What in tarnation is all this hullaba-loo?' Hartson muttered, stepping out into the dying rays of the sun. 'I sure hope that Iron Eyes ain't come back early for his horse.'

He stopped walking and gave out a huge sigh.

His eyes scrunched up amid the wrinkles that covered his face as he stared down to where the sound of panicking females rang out. He could see something but had no idea what it was at first. Then he heard another noise.

A noise which he had not heard for over ten years.

He raised a hand against the low sun and tried to see what it was that was causing so much distress. Dust billowed off the dry street at the opposite end of the town as whatever it was passed the saloon.

Hartson grabbed the arm of one of the men who were fleeing blindly. He jerked the man to a temporary halt. 'What you running from, Bert?'

'There's a damn stagecoach headed into town,' the elderly, man replied. Then he continued to defy his years by resuming his flight. 'The Devil himself is up on its driver's board.'

'That sure don't make no sense,' Hartson said, and rubbed his muscular neck thoughtfully. He then rested a broad shoulder against the wall of his livery and watched as the stagecoach cleared the dust. It was impossible for his tired eyes to see who was driving the stagecoach but the blacksmith was certain it was not the Devil.

The team of six lathered-up horses were thundering towards the tall livery building. Hartson shook his head.

'A stagecoach? He sure must be plumb lost,' he said. He shrugged and returned into the depths of the livery stable. 'Ain't bin a stagecoach come to Silver Creek in five or ten years. Yep. He's lost OK.'

Hartson walked back to the handsome stallion. He rested his knuckles on his hips and studied his handiwork. The animal was no longer in distress and that was the start of the animal's recovery. All the horse needed was rest but Hartson knew that its master was a man who did not care to rest his mounts.

'Thirsty, boy?' Hartson asked the horse. He picked up a bucket. 'I'll go get you some nice fresh cool water from the trough outside.'

The large man turned and saw the stagecoach come to a grinding halt right outside his wide-open stable doors. Clouds of dust billowed over the large vehicle.

Hartson walked towards it with the bucket in his right hand. When he reached the open air he heard the sound of a Winchester being cocked and readied for action.

The large man stopped.

He stared at the long barrel as it was levelled at him.

'You aiming a rifle at me?' Hartson's deep voice boomed out angrily. 'I don't like folks that aim guns at me. I've bin known to tear them apart with my bare hands. Savvy?'

The dust cleared from the driver's box.

The final rays of sunlight caught the long barrel of the rifle. It was still aimed down at the large liveryman.

'Big talk don't scare me none,' a voice growled from behind the Winchester. 'I killed a lot of critters with this toothpick and I ain't feared of anyone, no matter how fat they are.'

'Fat?' The blacksmith repeated the word and then sucked in his large belly. 'Who you calling fat?'

'You.'

The outraged blacksmith dropped the bucket angrily. 'I ain't fat. I'm just big. Get down from that bird branch and I'll rip your damn head off.'

'Fat men are always real touchy.' There was a hint of amusement in the voice. A voice which suddenly did not sound as masculine as it had.

Hartson tilted his head back and absorbed the words. He vainly tried to see who was holding the rifle but it was impossible as the rifle tracked his every movement.

'Hold on there a minute. Say that again,' he demanded.

'Why?'

A smile filled the bearded face. 'You can't fool me with all that tough talk. You're a gal. Either that or you're a man with a mighty big problem.'

Suddenly without any warning the Winchester blasted into action.

A blinding white plume of smoke and a deafening flash of lethal lead erupted from the end of the rifle barrel. A white-hot bullet came seeking the liveryman. His smile evaporated.

Hartson was knocked backwards.

His enormous frame landed on to the ground like a felled tree. Dust rose from all around his massive form as the small figure leapt down from the side of the stagecoach with the smoking carbine clutched in her small hands.

'Reckon that'll learn you. It don't pay to poke fun at Squirrel Sally,' the youthful voice warned. 'It don't pay nothing but a whole heap of pain.'

The blacksmith groaned as he forced himself up into a sitting position. He felt the graze burning across the top of his head and then stared at the blood on his fingertips. His bearded face was no longer smiling. Now there was the look of an angry grizzly bear carved in his weathered features.

'Ya shot me,' he shouted.

'I could have killed you,' Sally

replied. She pushed down the hand guard of the rifle and expelled a brass casing from its magazine. She jerked the lever back up and aimed straight at the blacksmith's head. 'I should have killed you.'

Hartson's eyebrows rose. He was staring down the barrel of a well-maintained repeating rifle and had no doubt that its owner knew how to use it.

'What you want to kill me for?'

The hot metal barrel drew closer to his face. Gunsmoke curled from the hole at its end.

'Why? You done killed my man, that's why.' Squirrel Sally was having to fight the demons within her soul not to pull on the Winchester's trigger a second time. 'You killed Iron Eyes.'

Hartson gasped. 'What?'

'You heard me, fat man,' Sally growled. 'You probably got his stinking carcass buried around this dung heap someplace.'

'He ain't dead,' the livery-stable

owner protested. He managed to force his hefty frame off the dirt until he was able to lean against the open door.

Squirrel Sally hit him in his belly with the rifle. 'Then how come you got his horse? His prized horse. Nobody could ever get their hands on that lump of glue unless Iron Eyes was dead.'

Hartson held his hands up as blood dripped from the graze on his scalp. 'Look at the critter. He's lame. Iron Eyes left the thing here for me to tend whilst he went hunting some outlaw.'

The tiny female snorted.

'He'd never leave that horse anyplace,' she fumed. 'He likes that yella nag better than me and I'm his woman.'

'Why would Iron Eyes like a horse better than you, gal?'

Sally thought for a moment. 'Maybe it's because the horse never shot him like I done.'

'That makes sense.' Bo Hartson edged to an upturned barrel and rested his rump on it. He looked at the small creature who held the rifle like a seasoned gunslinger as she paced to the palomino and back. 'He hired one of my saddle horses and went off towards the forest yonder. He'll be back as soon as he gets his hands on the outlaw he's chasing.'

Sally walked right up to the seated man, grabbed his side whiskers and tugged until she had a view of the man's scalp. She then released his whiskers.

'You'll live. Just a graze,' she announced.

'So you shot Iron Eyes as well?' Hartson asked.

'That was before we got betrothed,' Sally said.

'Betrothed?'

Squirrel Sally looked at the red sky above Silver Creek and gave out a long sigh. 'Yep. I'm his woman and he's my man.'

'If'n you two are betrothed then how come you ain't travelling with him?' Hartson dared to ask. 'He seemed in a mighty big rush to get out of town and head on up into the old forest. Can't recall him even mentioning you.'

The last of the day's fiery crimson rays covered the small bare-footed female as she stood with the smoking rifle in her capable hands. She looked as though the Devil himself had painted her from head to foot in his favourite hue.

'What?' Her eyes burned into the seated man.

'Nothing.' Bo Hartson shrugged and looked away. He did not want to get shot again. 'I never said nothing.'

6

Iron Eyes had been wrong. There were in fact fourteen riders in the wolf pack which had thundered across the rolling hills with their guns blazing at the bounty hunter. The horsemen had gathered in the very heart of the campsite around the scene of death and destruction and within moments had dismounted and started to rid the area of the bloodstained corpses. One after another they threw the dead bodies down the hillside and watched them pile up near the edge of the river, as their leader commanded.

They all knew exactly what had occurred here but none would ever willingly tell anyone else the truth. This had been, as Iron Eyes had guessed, an exercise in how to steal. It had been achieved at a tremendously high cost, but it had succeeded.

The leader of the riders stood beside the camp-fire and said nothing as his underlings continued to clean up the area all around them.

There was something mean about Major Tyler McGee. He never showed any emotion apart from anger. He gave orders and others obeyed; if they did not he killed them. For he worked for faceless creatures back East and it was their money that he controlled. Their orders were never questioned and he did not allow the riders whom he in turn hired to question him.

There was a fortune to be made and McGee had already managed to carve out for himself a tidy chunk of it. He remained like a statue as the last of the bodies were disposed of and the men turned their attention to feeding the fire in front of him with kindling.

Yet McGee was concerned.

Something had gone very wrong and the ex-military man knew it. Although the lumberjacks had all been killed by his men disguised as Indians, McGee had seen the lone rider flee from the scene as he had led the second wave of his attack on the camp.

Who was that rider?

The question burned into the major's mind.

How had all of his men been killed by others more used to swinging axes than firearms? The question festered as McGee remained beside the campfire beneath the black star-filled sky.

Major McGee did not look anything like most army officers, apart from the few who gained notoriety for their flamboyant appearance as well as their military prowess. He was what most men in the Wild West called a 'dude'.

He appeared elegant beyond what might be expected in a man of his rank. He had no fewer than three gunbelts wrapped around his still slim figure and dark-blue tunic. One belt was wrapped around his shoulders with its holstered weapon under his left arm, whilst two other belts crossed over his waist, leaving a gun on each hip. None of the guns was concealed by the regular army holster: their gun grips were exposed in readiness for a quick draw. McGee even carried a gun held by a neck chain, which dangled across the front of his pearl-buttoned vest.

Even his horse was well-armed with various types of rifles held in scabbards attached to its saddle.

Major Tyler McGee was a man who did everything to excess and that included killing. That had made him the first choice for his current paymasters back in Boston. Even a court martial had done nothing but make McGee even more wanted by the men who knew he could do what no honest man would do.

McGee could steal an entire forest for them. Steal it and have it sent downriver to those who waited for the countless felled trees.

Before anyone, including the true owners of the timber, knew what had happened the valuable trees would have floated along the waterway and been turned into a fortune in cash.

Yet the scene which had greeted McGee and his hired gunmen as they approached the campsite was not how it was meant to be. There had been an explosion which had accounted for most of the gunmen he had sent disguised as Indians.

The deep crater near the camp still smouldered. The scent of death still hung on the air, and that confused McGee. Who had caused the explosion?

Had it been the lone rider?

If so, who or what was he?

Major McGee had caught the briefest of glimpses of the rider a moment before the smoke and dust had obscured him as the fourteen horsemen had closed in upon what remained of the lumberjacks' campsite. What McGee had seen had troubled the disgraced cavalry officer.

For what he had seen had barely looked human. Whoever the rider was he had certainly not been one of the burly men who worked at cutting down vast forests.

McGee brooded.

The fleeing horseman had looked more like a skeleton.

Three of McGee's hand-picked men dropped piles of wood on to the fire and looked at their leader. They had all noticed the strange silence in the man who liked to hear the sound of his own voice barking out orders.

Kansas John Smith was the oldest of the bunch and had a respect for the man who stared into the flames. Angus Flagg was known for his ability with both six-shooter and rifle. It was said he never missed anything he aimed at. Then there was Preacher Bill who never ventured anywhere without his well-thumbed Bible. He was one of those men who always managed to justify the most brutal of his actions by finding a paragraph among its pages that, he claimed, gave him licence to kill.

'You sure are quiet, Major,' Smith noted as he pulled out his pipe. He placed it in the corner of his mouth, where a few teeth still remained amid a lot of gum. 'How come?'

'Yeah, you seem to be troubled, Major,' Flagg added. 'I would have reckoned that the job is done just like you planned. We got the timber and that's what we wanted.'

'What happened to all the boys we sent in dressed up as Injuns?' Preacher Bill asked aloud. 'We found Dooley but none of the other boys.'

McGee tilted his head towards Preacher Bill. 'Hell, that's easy. Someone managed to set off a wagon loaded with explosives down the trail. I think the blast did for the whole lot of them apart from Dooley.'

Smith scratched a match and cupped its flame over his pipe bowl. He sucked and then looked hard into the face of their leader. 'But something is gnawing at you, Major. We done what we was paid to do but you ain't happy. What's wrong?'

McGee straightened up. He had a

spine as straight as a measuring stick. 'Who was the rider?'

The men looked at McGee.

'I didn't see no rider,' Flagg said.

'That's because you were riding at the back of the pack, Flagg.' McGee rubbed his chin. 'All anyone could have seen from back there was dust.'

Flagg nodded. 'That's mighty true.'

Preacher Bill bit his lower lip. 'Come to think on it, I seen something riding across our path as we got within spitting distance of this camp. I thought it was a stray horse.'

Smith puffed on his smoke. 'I seen a rider for the smallest of time. Then he was gone in the smoke.'

McGee inhaled. 'I saw someone or something. He was headed towards the tree line. I fired a few shots at him but then he disappeared.'

'What you mean by 'something'?' Smith probed. 'You make it sound like you saw something that weren't natural, Major.'

Major MacGee gave a muted chuckle.

'I reckon it does but that's what I saw. Something that I can't say was a real man like you and me. Someone who looked more like a dead man than a living one.'

The three men fell silent.

7

The flames from the campfire were beginning to die down as the gunfighters sat around it finishing their supper. The aroma of hog fat still lingered as men washed down their food with their ration of hard liquor. Their leader had neither sat down or eaten anything during the previous half-hour. He had walked, through the darkness, around the boundaries of the camp, sucking on his high-priced cigar. The men had watched Tyler McGee disappear away from the light of the fire and only knew where he was by the glowing tip of his cigar. Then McGee turned and paced back to them across the blood-stained sand.

'We gonna make camp, Major?' one of the younger gunmen asked as the long legs of their leader passed by his shoulder. 'I'm real tuckered.'

'Me too,' another said.

Smoke drifted from McGee's mouth as he came to a halt next to the charred edges of the once blazing fire. His highly polished boots kicked at the cinders thoughtfully. McGee tapped the ash from his expensive cigar and studied each of his lethal men in turn.

'We have a long way to go before we bed down for the night, men,' McGee said through the smoke of his cigar. 'It might be dark but this day has a long way to go for us.'

Angus Flagg rubbed the grease of his supper off on his chaps and screwed up his eyes. He stared hard at the well-groomed officer who stood among them.

'But all we got left to do is get them logs moving down the river,' Flagg said. 'That'll wait until sunrise.'

McGee darted a rapier glance at Flagg. The fury in his eyes could be seen as the light of the flames danced in them.

'Well pardon me all to hell. Since when have you been the one who gives the orders, Angus?' McGee's tone was low and threatening. 'You don't bed down until I tell you it's OK.'

None of them argued.

Again McGee surveyed the seated men. What remained of his men were all hand-picked and knew how to obey the man who paid their wages. There was not one backbone between them, he thought. That was good for it meant they never contradicted him.

Flagg shrugged. 'What's wrong, Major? I didn't mean for you to think that I was giving any orders. I just figured . . . '

'I do the figuring, Angus.' McGee snapped.

'Yep. That's right. You do the figuring OK,' Flagg agreed.

Kansas John Smith wiped his mouth across his jacket sleeve and then scratched his chin.

'Ain't you gonna have some vittles, Major?'

'No,' McGee answered. His voice was cold. Like ice.

'You look troubled,' Preacher Bill noted. 'Why you looking so troubled, Major? We all thought this was over.'

'What else is there for us to do?' Flagg yawned. 'Dooley and the boys done for them lumberjacks.'

A few of the other men grunted in agreement with Flagg.

McGee took another long draw on his cigar before pointing at the forested mountainside. 'I don't think any of us can afford to sleep this night, men. Not with a stinking witness up there on the loose.'

Every one of the men looked up at McGee.

Kansas John Smith was first to speak. 'What you mean by that, Major? How can some yella belly give us any grief?'

'Whoever that was, he rode up into the trees, Kansas,' McGee replied. 'It dawned on me that we cannot afford to let him escape. He can tell the authorities what happened here. He can tell them that the Indian attack was not really an Indian attack at all, that it was a trick.'

'Who can spill the beans on us, Major?' Preacher Bill asked.

'The rider who high-tailed it.' Kansas John got to his feet and stood beside their leader. 'The Major is right. That varmint could get us all neck-stretched. It don't matter none if them redskins kill a whole heap of white folks but if white folks kills white folks them nosy bastards back East get interested.'

'Exactly.' McGee nodded. 'And our paymasters do not want awkward questions being asked. All they want is for a few million trees to end up in their sawmills.'

Flagg got to his feet. 'Are you sure you seen a rider fleeing to them trees, Major?'

The question was answered with the back of McGee's clenched left fist. Flagg staggered from the powerful blow and rocked on his boots as blood dripped from his mouth. He did not retaliate but turned away from the eyes of his comrades.

'Get up. You've had your food and your whiskey ration,' McGee ordered, raising his voice. 'The horses are now rested. Saddle them up and make sure your guns are primed. Now.'

The men got to their feet. They shuffled to their mounts and began to saddle them again.

'Hey, Major. You reckon that rider was one of these lumberjacks?' Kansas John asked.

McGee shook his head.

'No. He wasn't one of them,' McGee said through a cloud of cigar smoke. 'That's what worries me, Kansas. We don't know who or what he is. He might be a federal marshal for all we know. That sort of man is very dangerous.'

'I'll hurry the boys up,' Kansas John said. 'The sooner we catch and kill that critter the better off we'll all be.'

'Exactly.' McGee gripped the cigar

between his teeth and drew on its smoke thoughtfully. The deadly ex-military man watched while his most trusted hired gun joined the others as they threw saddles up on the backs of their horses.

Then Major McGee turned once more. His eyes stared at the trees bathed in the eerie starlight. The elegant man hated loose ends and the brief glimpse of Iron Eyes had fuelled his anger until it was festering inside him like a cancer. It gnawed at his guts and would not stop until he had finished off the bounty hunter once and for all.

'Think you've escaped, stranger?' McGee whispered through the cigar smoke. 'Well, you haven't. You're riding a tired horse but my horses are rested, fed and watered. Whoever you are I'll make sure you die before sunrise. I'll dance on your worthless body before you can inform anyone about what happened here.'

The baying of a distant wolf echoed

around the campsite as though even the wild animals of the forest knew what was about to invade their territory.

Death was coming in the guise of fourteen horsemen.

8

The brawny blacksmith had never before felt quite so helpless as he did in the company of the small female with the cocked Winchester still clutched in her hands. Bo Hartson hung another lantern from a nail and blew out the match he had just used to light its wick. Nervously he walked slowly to his forge and reached up for its long wooden lever. His muscular left arm pumped the forge vigorously sending red embers up into the crude but efficient metal chimney which was suspended above the glowing coals. Crimson light glowed across the watchful face of Squirrel Sally.

'How long do you figure on staying here, Squirrel?' Hartson asked. 'I'd have thought that you would have set out after Iron Eyes by now if you really intend catching up with him.'

She looked out at the dark street, then tilted her head back to stare at the stars. A thousand thoughts flashed through her young mind. Her eyes went back to the liveryman, whom she still did not trust.

The man who, she still thought, might have killed her beloved Iron Eyes and buried him somewhere in Silver Creek.

'I'll wait until sunup,' she retorted.

'Why?' Hartson walked towards her but stopped when she raised the barrel of the deadly rifle and aimed at him again. He had already tasted its venom and had no desire to repeat the painful experience. 'He's your man. You have to catch up with him, gal. You're wasting a lot of time staying here.'

'I ain't dumb, fat man. You just want to get rid of me.' Sally spat and smiled when she saw her spittle hit his boot.

Hartson inhaled deeply. 'Kind of. You make me nervous.'

Her smile widened. 'So you *can* tell

the truth when you have a mind, fat man.'

'Can you stop calling me fat? My name's Bo, Squirrel.' Hartson said.

'And my name ain't Squirrel,' Sally told him angrily. 'Only Iron Eyes calls me Squirrel. My name's Sally. Savvy?'

Hartson nodded. 'Yep. Reckon we understand one another.'

'So you say that my man took one of your saddle horses to follow an outlaw up into the forest?' Sally repeated the words the livery-stable owner had uttered many times since her abrupt arrival.

Hartson nodded again. 'Yep. A brown gelding.'

'Reckon I ought to hire one of your nags if I'm headed into that damn forest,' Squirrel Sally said thoughtfully. 'Reckon that place ain't suited for stagecoaches.'

'So you finally believe that I didn't kill Iron Eyes.' Bo Hartson sighed thankfully.

'Maybe,' Squirrel said. 'The thing is

that if I don't find his trail I'll know you was lying and I'll have to come back to kill you.'

The blacksmith swallowed hard. He knew she meant it. 'Are you good at tracking, Sally?'

'Yep.'

'Thank the Lord for that small mercy, Sally gal.' Hartson rubbed his neck.

The young woman wandered to his saddle horses in their stalls and studied them in turn. She had already forced Hartson to unhitch her six-horse team from their traces and put them in his corral.

'Not a bad-looking bunch,' she complimented.

'There are trails folks say are good enough for big vehicles like a stage,' the blacksmith observed. 'But if you want to make time then I reckon a saddle horse is the best choice.'

Sally lowered the rifle. 'I'll let you cut one out for me and you can lend me a saddle to go with it.'

Hartson thought about the money Iron Eyes had given him. It was more than enough to cover the cost of another horse and gear. He gave a nod.

'OK, Sally. It'll be my pleasure to lend you anything you want. Free of charge. I trust you. You could head on out in about ten minutes if I really work fast and get one of these gluepots saddled up for you.'

Squirrel Sally raised her eyebrows suspiciously. 'I told you. I ain't going no place until sunup, Bo. Can't track nothing in the dark if there ain't no moon.'

Hartson waved his hands.

'You're right. I'm sorry.'

She moved towards him. For such a small creature Sally had a way of frightening even the biggest of men. Hartson backed away from her.

She paused, looked at the man who towered over her and bit her lip.

'You got any vittles?'

He shook his head. 'Nope. I always go down to the café and get my grub.'

'I'm sure hungry,' Sally said, rubbing her stomach. 'I'm too tuckered to go out looking for something to shoot and skin for supper.'

'I could go get us some grub, gal,' Hartson ventured, then sniffed at the air. 'I can smell chicken cooking. Old Mary cooks mighty fine vittles and she always rustles up a couple of fat hens for my supper. Shall I shuffle off and go get us some and bring it back?'

'Nope.' Sally said as she turned and walked back towards the open doors of the livery. 'We'll go together and sit us down on some fancy chairs with a table. C'mon, Bo. I'm paying.'

'You got money?'

'Sure. I still got bounty money left from a bunch of outlaws me and Iron Eyes killed,' the youngster quipped.

'That's nice.' The huge blacksmith shrugged. He realized how close he had come to having his head blown off his shoulders and it made his knees feel weak.

Sally put the rifle over her shoulder

106

and marched out of the stable. 'How's your head?'

'It's stopped bleeding.'

'Good.'

Like an obedient puppy the large blacksmith followed her out into the dark street. The aromatic scent of frying chicken filled the air. They headed straight towards it and the café.

9

The forest had not changed for a thousand years or more. Its wolves still howled their chilling warnings all around the high trail as the bounty hunter steered his mount ever upwards along the narrow pathway. It was a reminder to Iron Eyes of his early life. The forest had always been filled with dangerous creatures but now with their habitat so greatly reduced there were far more of them to the square inch.

Iron Eyes eased himself up in his stirrups and listened as the painted pony nervously climbed the perilous track. The roar of cougars mingled with so many other animals filled the air. They were all close, he thought. Too damn close. At any moment a pack of rabid timber wolves might spring out of the dense brush from all sides and bring him and his mount down. Or the low-hanging branches might conceal a ravenous mountain lion, ready to leap down and kill him. He had seen how these creatures killed their prey many times. He had learned many things from them. To survive was to kill in this rugged place. There was no emotion in any of the animals who lived off the weaker creatures in the midst of this forest. Just as he had never shown any emotion when he had dispatched outlaws who were wanted dead or alive, Iron Eyes understood the need for the survival of the fittest.

To kill or be killed.

It had always been that simple.

He spurred on. The forest grew ever darker the higher Iron Eyes travelled up the clay pathway towards the clearing he recalled from his youth. There was fresh spring water there and he knew that the horse beneath his ornate saddle was flagging and in need of a drink.

He spurred his mount and forced it to continue towards the unknown. The darkness did not trouble the bounty hunter. Since he had been temporarily blinded a few months earlier his other senses had become keenly honed.

He looked all around him. Every shadow seemed to be of a different shade. The dim light showed everything from the smallest object to the largest. So far there had been nothing to alert him to draw either of his weapons. He knew there were thousands of deadly animals in the forest but so far they had kept their distance.

Perhaps it was the smell of death that the bounty hunter carried with him which kept them at bay. Maybe it was the sight of the hideous scarred face which confused even the most ravenous of them. There were a lot of things far more appetizing than his emaciated carcass.

Yet Iron Eyes knew that he dare not become complacent, for some animals killed for the sheer pleasure of it, never even desiring to feast upon their victims. His eyes darted and searched the gloom for any hint of danger.

As he sought it, Iron Eyes was fully aware that countless other eyes were also watching his slow progress through their domain. Then the warning sounds of wolves baying mixed with the hunting calls of nocturnal birds as they swooped expertly through the trees without ever colliding with any of them alerted his keen instincts. Iron Eyes was home. After so many years of travelling and killing he had returned to the one place where his scarred features meant nothing.

This was home.

His home.

The sanctuary he knew like the back of his bony hands.

Yet no matter how hard Iron Eyes tried he could not recall ever being anything but alone in this place. Perhaps he had been a mistake, abandoned, then, against all the odds, had somehow survived.

Whatever the truth it would remain buried in the past.

Shafts of dim starlight managed to

cut down through the gloom from small gaps in the dense canopy far above him, but it was his memory which was guiding him now. He kept heading upwards in search of the clearing he remembered from so long ago.

His thoughts drifted.

He recalled that long ago he had fought with many Indians in this place. There seemed to be no sign of them any longer. He sniffed at the air like a wild animal vainly trying to capture the scent of distant-cooking. He remembered how he had stolen many meals from Indians as a youngster, but there was no aromatic aroma of cooking any longer.

It seemed strangely unnerving to the thin horseman.

Where were the natives who had once filled this vast, untamed terrain?

Had the men who had destroyed so much of the forest also wiped out the men, women and children who had lived within its confines since time began?

Iron Eyes grew angry.

Most men from the outside world would kill one another just for the sheer pleasure of it. Add a fortune in timber and not one of the Indians would have been safe from those determined to get their hands upon it. It seemed insane but he knew it was true.

In all the years that he had roamed this wilderness he had always known when the Indians were near. He had always been able to sense their presence, but not now.

Iron Eyes spurred again.

Had the lumberjacks or those who fought with them wiped out an entire community of people?

Iron Eyes shuddered at the thought. The pony responded to his spurs and kept heading upwards along the muddy clay trail. He jerked the reins to his left. He knew the trail forked round a crippled tree with double-barrelled trunks. He tapped his spurs; the horse jumped over an exposed root and landed firmly on one of the two tracks.

He eased the reins to his right and proceeded onwards. Iron Eyes knew that although the trail he had chosen appeared to be heading downhill, it would in fact take him up through a dense wooded area before reaching the clearing.

Then without warning the painted pony suddenly and violently bucked, refusing to go any further. The bounty hunter was caught by surprise. The horse dropped its head and then, like a rebellious mule, began to buck. Its hind legs kicked out at the darkness. Over and over again the snorting animal repeated its action.

Iron Eyes suddenly realized that he was no longer sitting on his saddle but flying through the air over the bowed head of the horse. Before he knew it the thin rider had crashed through a dense tangle of bushes and was stopped by the well-hidden tree trunk. Dazed, Iron Eyes felt the long leathers slipping through his fingers as his mount backed away.

'Hold on, you damn gluepot!' Iron Eyes threw himself backward and caught hold of the reins. He wrapped them around his bony wrists and was then tugged off his feet. It took every ounce of his strength to stop the horse from escaping. He felt the clay beneath his pants as his skinny frame was dragged twenty or more feet back down the trail. Only the spikes of his large spurs enabled him to slow his progress. Slow him enough for him to wrap the long leathers around a sturdy sapling. Somehow Iron Eyes managed to tie a knot in the reins. His scarred face screwed up as his hands knotted the leathers until they held firm.

Covered from head to boot in damp clay Iron Eyes staggered to his feet whilst the horse continued to snort and buck as it fought with its restraints.

Furiously Iron Eyes pulled one of his guns from a coat pocket, cocked its hammer and aimed it at the horse's head. His sharp teeth gritted.

'Reckon I ought to learn ya some

manners,' he snarled while the horse continued to buck up and down on the narrow trail. 'I reckon I ought to part ya hair so you'll not go throwing me off again.'

The horse kept fighting furiously with the reins that held it in check. It was snorting louder and louder as terror gripped its soul.

'Will you shut the hell up?' the bounty hunter yelled.

The horse continued to fight with the reins. The sapling began to bend.

Exasperated, Iron Eyes kicked out at the animal. His long thin legs missed their target. Then the bounty hunter looked back up the trail to where he had been thrown so ignominiously. He noticed a shaft of eerie starlight illuminating the tree-lined trail.

Then Iron Eyes saw something.

'What is that?' he muttered, a heartbeat before he heard branches rustling. His eyes narrowed and focused on the trees that graced both sides of the path. Their topmost branches, like

116

so many others in the forest, had interwoven, allowing anything beneath their canopy to move unhindered from one tree to another without having to come down to earth.

The starlight caught a slender, graceful black shadow as it moved along the branches from one tree to the next. Then a spine-chilling roar filled the air.

'Holy cow!' Iron Eyes kept the Navy Colt aimed at the puma as its head turned. It looked through the branches and leaves straight at the startled man. The yellow eyes of the big cat burned across the distance between them. It studied the horse and its master.

'A lion. A mighty big'un at that.'

The frightened horse kept on battling with the long leathers that held it in check. Giving out a pitiful whinny it reared up behind the bounty hunter and frantically lashed out with its hoofs. Both caught Iron Eyes in his back. He arched and was sent hurtling to the ground. No sooner had the emaciated figure crashed into the mud then the Navy Colt in his hand blasted. A blinding plume of fury was unleashed from its barrel as the stunned bounty hunter lay on his face.

Then the noise of the puma's growling grew even louder. Iron Eyes forced himself up and saw the lithe animal leap down to the ground. The shot had not scared it away; it had actually enraged it and caused it to attack.

It moved fast.

Faster than he would have imagined possible.

Iron Eyes spat the mud from his mouth and cocked the guns hammer again, but it was too late.

The big cat sprang.

The thin man was hit hard by the pouncing creature. So hard that he was knocked off his knees by the sheer weight of the puma. A flash of the long claws which narrowly missed Iron Eyes were lit up by another fruitless shot. The bruised man slid on his back across the clay trail until his head collided with a tree trunk.

Dazed and confused Iron Eyes managed to cock his gun and fire again. The flash from the shot lit up the trail for a brief moment. It was long enough for the stunned bounty hunter to see that yet again he had missed his target.

The puma gave out a terrifying growl.

He had never known a big cat so fearless before and it chilled the injured Iron Eyes to the bone. He desperately clawed at his gun hammer again, whilst the ferocious animal prowled around the narrow trail. The pony was now foaming at the mouth as it tried vainly to break free of its restraints but it was not the horse that the mountain cat wanted.

It was Iron Eyes.

The bounty hunter was about to move, then suddenly he realized that half of his coat and shirt front had been torn from his thin body. The starlight traced across his hand as he stared at the blood on his fingers. Even the eerie forest darkness could not hide his savaged flesh. Iron Eyes had not realized until this moment that the puma had ripped his skin almost from his chest.

'This ain't good,' he muttered as he stared out at the baleful yellow eyes of his adversary. 'Why ain't you scared?'

In all his days he had never known a puma that was not a coward at heart. Usually any sudden noise would send them on their way, but not this one. This one was different. A terrifying thought filled Iron Eyes' mind as the animal stopped and prepared for one last leap.

He was no longer the hunter.

Now he was the prey.

His hands tried feverishly to control the weapon in his muddy grip. It, like its master, had ploughed through the muddy clay as Iron Eyes had been knocked across the damp pathway. The Navy Colt had to be fully cocked before it could be fired, and that was proving to be impossible.

'C'mon, gun,' Iron Eyes snarled at the six-shooter as he tried to get a grip on its hammer. 'Don't let me down now. Not here. Damn it all.'

The puma paused as it studied its target. Then its body seemed to coil like a living spring, backward. It stopped. Iron Eyes watched the large tail sway like a snake while every sinew in the big cat grew taut.

'Damn!' Iron Eyes cursed.

The puma leapt again.

All Iron Eyes could do was watch as it flew through the air to where he lay crumpled against the tree. Time seemed to stand still as his muddy fingers tried to get the Navy Colt to fully cock.

Then the slippery gun fell from his hands. There was no time to drag its identical twin from the other deep coat pocket. No time to do anything but stare helplessly at the lethal claws, teeth and eyes of the puma as it leapt upon him.

10

Just before the needle-sharp claws of the springing beast hit the already stunned bounty hunter dead centre, Iron Eyes had heard a shot. A deafening shot which echoed all around the area as the flash from a rifle barrel illuminated the raging beast. The shot had come from somewhere behind and far above the attacking puma. The brief burst of light from the rifle shot had not lasted long but it had been long enough to show the defenceless Iron Eyes exactly what was attacking him. In all his days he had never seen such a large mountain cat. With claws extended the animal battered into the winded bounty hunter's chest. There was so much power, weight and strength in the attacking beast that Iron Eyes was pushed across the slippery ground and over the edge of the high trail. As his emaciated figure toppled down through the untamed brush and brambles he saw the lifeless body of the animal soar over his head and disappear into the gloom.

There was no time to celebrate for the man who was falling like a rag doll down through a wild terrain. He felt his long sticklike body crashing through the undergrowth and then the agony as he glanced off trees. It seemed to the half-conscious bounty hunter that his brutal descent was lasting for ever. Then it stopped. A stout tree set thirty feet below the high trail abruptly halted Iron Eyes.

Every last squeak of wind had been knocked out of his body.

His blood-covered frame was wrapped around the trunk of the tall pine tree, which grew a third of the way down the almost precipitous slope. Although he did not know it, the tree had saved Iron Eyes' life.

The suspended bounty hunter remained motionless for more than five minutes until his benumbed brain began to function again. Slowly he began to gather his thoughts together.

Then he sucked in air and forced his eyes open. He looked down at the lethal drop below him, then slowly began to disentangle himself from the tree trunk. Luckily for Iron Eyes the tree had grown straight. Tentatively in the gloomy starlight the severely injured man managed to get his boots on to the steep slope and rest his back against the tree trunk. He rested against it and studied the mass of dense vegetation that faced his blood-soaked body. Only then did the true magnitude of how far he had fallen dawn on Iron Eyes.

'Hell, that sure ain't something I'd want to do again,' Iron Eyes said as blood dripped from his mouth. He spat, screwed up his eyes and waited until he was able to focus accurately.

Balancing against the tree he tilted his head and stared down into the abyss. A fog swirled and heaved like a living beast below him. He knew that the mist hid deadly jagged boulders.

Iron Eyes straightened up and looked again at the mass of intertwined vines before him. He had to climb back to where he had left his horse, he told himself, yet a million grey shadows made it seem even more daunting that it actually was. If there was a way of getting back up to the high trail from where he was precariously perched, the bounty hunter could not see it.

'Damn it all!' he cursed, clenching both fists.

Vague shafts of starlight drifted on the air across the forest and settled upon his torso. He tilted his head forward and looked down. His mane of long hair hung over his blood-covered chest. He focused on the deep savage claw marks scored into his flesh and the glistening blood. His blood. It was still seeping from every wound.

He returned his eyes to the overhanging brush. Then he heard something far above him. He wanted to move to try and get a better view but knew that he dare not.

Another sound drew his attention. He strained to hear.

Then he heard something else. Bats flew away from the wall of green vegetation as a rope uncoiled before him. He leaned forward, gripped the rope and gave it a tug. It was secured firmly to something high above him.

Whoever had thrown the rope down was offering him a lifeline from the nightmare in which he was trapped. A way to escape from this perilous brink of doom.

'Who's up there?' Iron Eyes called out. His bony hands made a large loop in the end of the rope and placed it over his shoulders until it was under his armpits. He tightened the knot and held on to the rope.

There was no reply.

'Who the hell are you?' Iron Eyes whispered. 'And what you helping me for? I sure can't see no profit in it.'

It was time to move.

His long arms pulled down on the rope until every inch of its slack had reached his boots. He stepped closer to the brush and then began to haul his thin frame upward. Every sharp thorn seemed to find his face and body as he forced himself up though the enmeshed vines. He could feel even more of his skin being torn as he continued to drag himself higher and higher. His boots managed to take most of the strain as he thrust them into the soft earth in front of him. The vines were so strong that they acted like a crude rope ladder.

It was taking every ounce of his already depleted strength but Iron Eyes refused to give in. He was going to reach the end of the rope and find out who it was who seemed to want to help him survive.

The taste of blood still filled his mouth. His tongue could feel that his teeth were looser than they usually were. It did not pay to wrestle with a puma, he reasoned. He had to reach the trail and his horse and his saddle-bags and the whiskey bottles. He needed whiskey for more than the usual reason.

The climb grew harder. He seemed to be falling face first into the spiny undergrowth with each pull on the rope. He was panting like a stomped hound dog but knew he had to keep going.

There was no other way.

To stop now would be to fall back,

Even half dazed, Iron Eyes was still sharp enough to know that the next time he fell he might not be lucky enough to collide with the tree.

The next time he might just carry on falling or end up hanging like a puppet until the next ravenous creature found him and feasted upon his carcass.

'Keep going,' he told himself. 'Can't be much further.'

A score of thoughts filled his mind.

Who had shot the puma?

Why would they shoot the puma?

Who dropped the rope down to save him?

How had he managed to ride into a

crazy battlefield?

What was going on?

Had the wanted outlaw he had been hunting anything to do with any of this?

So many questions and not a single answer.

'I got to get back up to my horse,' Iron Eyes muttered as his bony hands kept on hauling his lightweight frame up the side of the steep wall of wild plants. 'I need me a long drink of my whiskey. A real big, long drink of my whiskey.'

The single thought of reaching his satchel of hard liquor and consuming it seemed to spur the exhausted bounty hunter on. He leaned back, holding the rope in his hands, and dug his boot toes into the mesh of vines. Within a few minutes he had covered another ten feet up the almost vertical hillside.

With each movement he made progress up the slippery slope until he could see the very spot where he had been thrust from the trail. It had been so close and yet so far away.

'Keep going, Iron Eyes,' he snarled to himself. 'Think of the whiskey. Think of that mighty fine whiskey.'

His pointed boot toes thrust into the soft surface of the hillside. The tangled vines were strong and refused to break as hand and boots used them as a crude ladder.

'Got to keep going,' Iron Eyes repeated over and over again so that his mind could fight the torturous pain which was ripping through his every sinew.

There was no quitting, he told himself.

To quit was to die.

Halfway up the treacherous slope Iron Eyes reached the carcass of the puma. It had followed him over the edge of the high trail but its dead body had become ensnared in a tangle of ivy that stretched around a trio of saplings. The body of the puma was suspended by the foliage.

Iron Eyes snarled at it as, with his bleeding hands he kept hauling himself up by the rope. As he passed the limp carcass of the puma his eyes darted and he gloated on its fate.

The eerie starlight enabled him to see the blood on the light-coloured fur just behind the animal's head. It had been a clean and deadly accurate shot that had killed the big cat. The bounty hunter smiled.

'That'll learn ya,' the bloody bounty hunter spat. 'It don't pay to mess with Iron Eyes. The Devil got himself a soft spot for me.'

He pressed on. The rope was now taut. He was reaching his goal. The bushes and vines on the edge of the high trail had not prevented him from being knocked over its rim but they were strong enough to take the weight of the thin blood-soaked man as he managed to drag himself up the last few feet.

Totally wearied, Iron Eyes lay on the flat muddy path and released the rope. He raised his head and looked through the limp strands of his mane of hair.

He had expected to see his saviour.

Whoever had thrown the rope down into the gully had tied it securely to a large tree but now was nowhere to be seen. He had gone and that troubled Iron Eyes.

The bounty hunter pushed his limp hair from his face, then saw his horse. It was still where he had left it tethered to the sapling.

His horse reared up again as the horrific figure managed to get to his feet. Iron Eyes' legs were shaking as they supported him but he did not notice. He wiped the mud off his hands down what was left of his coat front.

'Something don't add up here,' Iron Eyes muttered. He stepped into a thin beam of starlight and looked down at himself again. Blood and mud covered him. His shirt was in shreds and the front of his trail coat had fared no better. He looked at the deep claw marks that had torn his flesh very nearly to the bone and shook his head.

'Reckon I better try and find that

spring and clean up these wounds,' the bounty hunter muttered, adding: 'Damn. I'll have to waste even more whiskey cleaning up these cuts.'

He moved unsteadily back to the tree against which he had smashed the back of his skull and the pool of mud in which his gun lay. He rested a hand on the trunk of the tree, scooped up the weapon and dropped it into his deep coat pocket.

Iron Eyes paused for a moment. He drew in air and looked at the thicket of dense green brush which rose up further than he could see.

Where was the rifleman?

There seemed to be no sign of him but the hideous bounty hunter knew that the marksman had to be close: close enough to see everything that was going on. Close enough to take an unhindered shot and kill a leaping puma. Close enough to have killed him rather than the wild animal. He glanced at his saddle horn. It had been his own rope that the unknown man had used to rescue him.

Iron Eyes looked at his horse.

It was soaked in a fearful lather and was still rearing up.

The tall man staggered to it, grabbed at its bridle and pulled the horse's head close to his own. Horse and master were nose to nose, eyeballing one another.

'Listen up. The only reason I ain't blown your damn head off is that maybe you saved my life, horse.' Iron Eyes snorted and then bellowed. 'Maybe you saved my life but maybe your bucking spooked that damn mountain lion into attacking me. I ain't sure yet. Be very, very careful. I ain't in no mood to get thrown again. Savvy?'

The horse went silent.

It stopped fighting with the reins that had held it in check. Its head dropped.

Iron Eyes leaned on the saddle and pulled out one of his whiskey bottles. He drew its cork and took a long swig from its clear glass neck.

It tasted good.

Real good.

When he lowered the bottle something caught his eyes far below him. Iron Eyes took two shaking steps and halted.

His eyes narrowed as they focused on something far below.

Something which surprised and also troubled him.

Fiery torches were entering the forest. A lot of fiery torches. Iron Eyes rubbed his scarred chin and filled his mouth with more of the fiery whiskey. He swilled it around his loose teeth and swallowed.

'Damn it all!' He exhaled angrily, then had another more fleeting thought. 'Maybe they ain't after me. Them critters might be after more Injuns to kill.'

For a few moments the fourteen horsemen seemed to be at a standstill, as though they were unsure which way to go. Iron Eyes smiled. Then to his horror they chose the very trail he had taken to reach the place where he now stood. He watched as the line of torches began to ascend the trail.

Iron Eyes searched what was left of his inside coat pockets and pulled out a long, twisted cigar and a dry match. He watched the riders curiously as he placed the cigar in his bloody mouth.

The dishevelled man raised the match. 'Could be a coincidence, them taking the same trail as me.'

His thumbnail had no sooner flicked the top of the match and ignited it than he heard and saw their rifles explode into earth-shaking action.

A half-dozen red-hot tapers sped through the darkness and flew over his head. Calmly, Iron Eyes lit his cigar and blew the flame out.

'Nope. I was right the first time,' he sighed through a line of choking smoke as even more shots streaked up at him from the line of horsemen. 'They want to kill me, OK. They want my scalp even more than that damn puma did.'

He turned and staggered back to the horse. His bony left hand pulled the reins free, then he led the cowering animal further up the trail.

'This is turning out to be a real bad day,' Iron Eyes complained as despite his bleeding body, he managed to lead the painted pony higher up into the dense forest. 'A real bad one and no mistake.'

11

Darkness and a million stars hung over the remote settlement of Silver Creek as a thunderstorm lit up the sky away in the distance. The storm was slowly coming closer but in the middle of the night there were few to witness its approach, apart from Bo Hartson as he closed the big double doors of the livery against the night chill. His large figure moved through the lantern light and then sat down next to the warmth of his well-stoked forge. He gave the long wooden arm a few gentle tugs and relaxed as sparks flew upward through the chimney which hung over the glowing coals.

He lifted the coffee pot and gave it a shake. It was still half-full of the black beverage. He placed the pot in the very centre of the coals, and then turned to watch the small creature curled up in one of the horse stalls again. Even asleep Squirrel Sally Cooke looked dangerous.

She was snoring louder than most fully grown men but even quite asleep her hands never released their grip on her trusty Winchester. The liveryman gave her a smile as he filled his pipe bowl with tobacco and pressed it down with his thumb. He had not slept since they had returned to the livery stables after he and Sally had finished their meal in the café two hours earlier.

Like all youngsters, she had tried to stay awake even when she was utterly exhausted. Then, an hour earlier, she had finally lost her battle with the sandman and fallen into a deep slumber in one of the empty horse stalls.

For some reason he could not put his finger on, Hartson had actually grown to like the small female. She had more grit in her tiny body than most and that fared well with the big man. Yet unlike himself Sally was young. Far younger than she would ever admit to being and that amused him. The blacksmith watched her like hens watch their chicks. He wanted to protect her but something deep inside him desired something more. Something he knew he would never have.

He considered her words about the scarecrow of a bounty hunter, Iron Eyes, as he raised a set of hot tongs from the coals of the forge and carefully placed them over the bowl of his pipe. He sucked in the smoke, then quietly returned them to the place where they would remain until required again.

Hartson puffed on his pipe until a cloud of smoke hung over his head. Evidence of the bullet graze still showed across its hairless dome.

He wondered if Iron Eyes even knew that this young girl was hunting him in just the way that he hunted wanted outlaws. He also wondered if the infamous bounty hunter knew that she was claiming that they were betrothed.

He gave out a muted chuckle.

Maybe that was why Iron Eyes seemed so eager to continue on his quest even though his magnificent horse was lame. Was Iron Eyes afraid of Squirrel Sally?

Was that it?

Hartson laughed out loud.

This time it was enough to awaken the sleeping woman and bring her up into a sitting position with her trusty rifle gripped in her hands.

'What was that?' Sally asked. She blinked hard, trying to rid her eyes of the sleep that encrusted them. 'Did ya hear that, fat man?'

The blacksmith gave a slow nod. 'Yep. I heard it, Sally gal. It was me laughing.'

'Why was you laughing?' Sally sleepily rose from the hay and blew the hair from her face as she walked barefoot towards him. Her clothing was travel-worn. Like those of the man she hunted they were covered in the dirt and dried blood gathered over a hundred miles. Her shirt barely covered her upper body, yet she did not seem to notice or care. Her pants were torn from adventures that Hartson could only imagine.

He shrugged. 'No reason. I had me a thought and it just tickled me pink.'

Squirrel Sally stopped and stared at the seated man. He was taller than she, even when he was sitting down. Her head tilted as she lowered the rifle, grabbed his pipe and took herself a long suck on its stem. She then tossed the pipe back to him. The big man caught it and watched as she slowly exhaled the smoke.

'Are ya loco? I'd hate for me to be finding out I'm sharing a barn with someone who ain't got a whole deck of cards for his mind to play with.'

Hartson chuckled again and removed the pipe stem from his mouth. He aimed it at her.

'You are the strangest little gal I ever met, Sally.'

Her head straightened up on her slim neck. Her eyes narrowed as she studied the amused man.

'Me strange? I like that,' she snorted. 'I ain't the one who's laughing at jokes that nobody else can hear, fat man.'

He nodded. 'That's true. I mean you just ain't like none of the females I ever met before. The ones I used to see around Silver Creek were all cut from the same cloth. They all wanted to dress up fancy and act like they was special. Not you. You are what you are.'

She bent forward and glared at him. 'And what am I?'

'Wonderful,' Hartson chuckled. 'You are plumb wonderful, gal. Iron Eyes is a mighty lucky man having you as a fiancée.'

'What you call me?' Squirrel Sally thrust the rifle under his chin. The blacksmith roared with laughter until tears filled his eyes. He coughed and slapped his knee.

'It means betrothed, Sally gal,' he replied.

Sally raised an eyebrow in disapproving confusion. 'You are loco, fat man.

Plumb loco. *Feeansee?* There ain't no such word.'

He nodded. 'Ya right. I'm sorry. But Iron Eyes is sure lucky to have a fine gal like you.'

She nodded firmly. 'Damn right. He don't know how lucky he is. I sure wish he'd stop running away, though. Ain't easy for me to be hunting all over the place for him, ya know?'

Hartson stood. 'I know. Must be mighty annoying. After all a pretty little thing like you is rare. He just don't seem to have the wits to figure that.'

She gave a firm nod. 'Yeah. Mighty annoying. Anyone would think that he's scared of me. Just coz I shot him once.'

The liveryman lifted the blackened coffee pot off the forge and filled his tin cup. He took a sip, then looked at her. He cleared his throat and replaced the cup.

'Some men wouldn't run away from a lovely gal like you, Sally. Some men would be real proud of having such a wonderful female like you to love.'

Squirrel Sally stared hard at him. Then she saw the look in his eyes that she had noticed other men displaying when they encountered her.

'Easy, fat man. I seen that look before,' Sally said, pointing the barrel of her rifle at him. 'You got sap rising. I knows about these things. I seen bulls with the same dumb look in their eyes like you got. I also seen what them bulls do when they gets close to a cow. Take in some air and calm down.'

Hartson did as he was told. He inhaled deeply and then gave a sad shake of his head.

'Sorry, Sally gal. You're right. I don't get me much female company and you sure are the kind that can get a man's sap to rise. I'm only a man and you sure are a pretty little thing.'

Squirrel Sally looked stern. 'Control yourself and your damn sap. Now go get that saddle horse ready for me. I got me a bounty hunter to catch.'

Hartson stood, placed the cup down and turned towards the horses in their stalls. Then he stopped.

'Hold on just a minute. I thought you said that you wasn't headed out until dawn?'

She scratched her neck.

'I know what I said but I didn't figure on you falling in love with me. Makes it hard for a woman when a man goes all soft on her. Reckon I'd best head on out now before you do something I'll have to shoot you for doing. Savvy?'

The large man smiled.

'I savvy, Sally gal.'

Sally watched Hartson drag a saddle off a wall hook. She studied him long and hard. He was the most muscular man she had ever seen but he was old, she thought. Had to be close to forty or even more.

'Answer me something,' she said. 'Why do ya think men act funny after I shoot them, Bo?'

He roared with laughter again and shook his head. His tear-filled eyes looked at her through the smoke of the pipe gripped in his teeth.

'Hell. You are something special, little one.'

Squirrel Sally looked utterly confused. 'And you are just plumb loco. Real plumb loco. Get that horse saddled. Fast.'

The liveryman led out a saddle horse and patted it. 'There's a bad storm headed this way, Sally. Reckon it'll be mighty dangerous out there with lightning come down like rain. Are you sure you don't want to wait until dawn?'

The beautiful young woman ran a sleeve under her nose.

'I'll take my chances,' she said.

'But lightning can be lethal, Sally gal.' Hartson placed a blanket on the back of the horse. 'Real lethal.'

Sally pulled hay from her hair. 'Maybe I'd be scared if I knew what lethal means.'

'It means deadly, gal.' The blacksmith lifted up the saddle, positioned it perfectly on the horse's back, then reached under the animal's belly for the cinch straps. 'You know what deadly means?'

'Yep. It means sharing a barn with a lovesick fat man, Bo.' She winked.

Laughter boomed out of Hartson again.

12

With blazing torches held high the fourteen horsemen kept on riding up the narrow trail with Major Tyler McGee at their head. The higher they climbed the cooler the air seemed to get. Angus Flagg stood in his stirrups looking out through the trees to their right. He saw flashes of lightning through the close lattice-work of leafy branches.

'There's a storm headed this way, Major,' Flagg called out to their leader. 'Looks kinda mean to me.'

McGee glanced to where Flagg was pointing his rifle. He gave a nod of agreement and returned his eyes to what lay ahead of them.

Kansas John Smith moved his horse alongside the mount of Tyler McGee and looked at the stone-faced rider. He leaned across the distance between them.

'I can catch him, Major,' Smith announced. 'Whoever that *hombre* is up yonder, I can catch him for sure.'

McGee looked at the horseman beside him. The flickering light of their torches lit up his face.

'We're all going to catch up with him eventually, Kansas.'

'You don't understand. I mean I knows a way of getting in front of the varmint, sir.' Smith explained.

'How?' McGee asked.

'I know the lie of the land up there, Major.' Smith smiled. 'Me and Preacher Bill went up there a few weeks back as we kept an eye on the campsite for you. I know every damn tree up there and every damn short cut.'

'He's right, Major,' Preacher Bill said from behind the two riders. 'We had us a scuffle with a stray Injun but I did for the heathen. We know every tree stump up there.'

McGee concentrated on the steep trail which was unfamiliar to him. He tilted his head and looked back at the others. Each of their faces was glowing red in the torchlight. It was like looking at a pack of devils.

'What's up there?' the major asked.

'A clearing,' Smith replied. 'And a spring running into a creek. Hard to find unless you know where to look.'

'And we know where to look,' Preacher Bill snarled.

McGee was thoughtful. 'And you know how to get there before that rider does, Kansas?'

'Sure enough.' Smith nodded.

'We couldn't find no safe way out of there, Major.' Preacher Bill said. 'Once a man heads up there he has to backtrack to go anywhere else.'

McGee remained thoughtful. 'So he can be cornered in there?'

'Yep. I can trap and kill that varmint, Major.' Smith grinned. 'I found a way in there that I bet even the sweet Lord don't know about. I also know how to get there without sticking on this trail all the way.'

'But surely we could all get him

cornered?' McGee asked his right-hand man.

'Sure, but he'll see and hear the whole bunch of us coming,' Smith argued. 'Let me go on my lonesome and I might even get there before he does. Can I go, Major?'

McGee gave a nod. 'I want his head, Kansas. Whoever he is I want his head. Understand?'

'I'll get you his head, sir,' Smith said. 'On a pike.'

'Get going, Kansas. We shall continue on up the trail at a steady pace whilst you finish him off.' McGee spoke without any hint of emotion in his voice.

Kansas John spurred his horse and thundered away from the rest of the group. Preacher Bill eased his mount next to their leader and gave out a low chuckle.

'So you encountered an Indian whilst you were up there, Preacher?' McGee commented.

'Yep,' Preacher Bill grunted. 'A heathen.'

The riders kept on riding up the precarious pathway at a steady pace. The trees and bushes were closing in on the horsemen from both sides. Every turn was half-concealed by untamed vegetation. Few men had ever ridden past this point.

'Fall back, Preacher,' McGee ordered. 'The trail is getting narrower.'

Ignoring the order Preacher Bill gave out a flesh-crawling snigger as he leaned close to the major. 'You want to see my money pouch, Major? Made it myself.'

McGee looked at Preacher Bill. 'Why would I want to look at a money pouch? Fall back.'

The Bible-toting horseman leaned across even more closely and whispered. 'Why? Coz it's made from the hide of that heathen I told you about, Major. Ain't you interested?'

McGee's eyes widened. His head turned as he looked in disbelief at the man who claimed to be religious but in truth was little better than the worst of them. 'What? Did I hear you correctly, Preacher?'

'You sure did. When I killed that savage I cut me off a chunk of flesh and made me a money pouch from it,' Preacher Bill boasted. 'It's like a keepsake.'

'You killed an Indian warrior and then made yourself a pouch from his flesh?' McGee raged. 'That's disgusting.'

'That savage weren't no warrior, Major,' Preacher Bill corrected. 'It was just a squaw. You know what else I done to her after I slit her throat?'

Tyler McGee could not hide the revulsion that was brewing inside him. For the first time for years he felt true anger deep inside his normally impassive soul.

'A female? You killed and then mutilated a female?'

'Sure enough.' Preacher Bill smiled. 'You want to see it? Looks just like pig leather.'

McGee returned his eyes to the trail

ahead of them. For the first time the torchlight revealed emotion on his countenance. It was revulsion. Total revulsion.

'You sicken me,' the major seethed. 'You're the savage, not some innocent female. You are the mindless heathen. Not her.'

'She was nothing but an Injun,' Preacher Bill snarled.

'And you are the savage,' McGee snarled back.

'I don't have to listen to no insults from the likes of you, Major.' Preacher Bill gave a snorting grunt and spurred his mount furiously. The horse galloped away from the rest of McGee's men along the dangerous trail.

The major raised himself in his stirrups.

'Get back here, Preacher,' McGee yelled out loudly. 'That's an order. Do you hear me? Get back here.'

'You know what you can do with your orders, Major,' Preacher Bill shouted out and kept thrusting his spurs into the flanks of his horse. He did not bother to look back as he rode after Kansas John Smith. 'Nobody talks to the Preacher like that. I ain't no heathen. I'm a white man.'

Flagg trotted away from the other horsemen until he was riding next to the dumbfounded McGee.

'You want me to ride after the Preacher and bring him back, Major?' Flagg asked.

The major narrowed his eyes and glared up into the eerie darkness ahead of them.

'No, Angus. That won't be necessary.' McGee patted the rider on the back. 'Some men are not worth chasing. We can only hope Preacher Bill gets everything the Lord throws down at him.'

'Reckon so, sir. Reckon so.' Flagg nodded. 'I can hear that storm growing louder, sir.'

McGee looked heavenward. 'How long before you think it will reach the forest, Angus?'

'Less than an hour by my figuring,' Flagg guessed.

'I hope that we are out of this forest by then,' McGee said in a concerned tone. 'I certainly do not relish trying to ride down this trail after a storm has soaked its surface.'

'Me neither,' Flagg agreed. 'This trail ain't nothing more than clay by my reckoning. Ain't nothing worse than to try to ride down a wet clay trail.'

'Indeed.' McGee raised an arm and then signalled. 'Double pace, men. Double pace.'

The dozen riders spurred up the hazardous trail as brief flashes of lightning lit up the sky far above the trees in warning of what was yet to come.

13

Silver Creek was a long way behind the intrepid Squirrel Sally and getting further away with each stride of the muscular gelding that Bo Hartson had provided her with. The stars had all but vanished in the angry heavens as clouds fought high above the ravaged land that had once been the major part of a forest.

Draped in the long undertaker's frock-coat that Iron Eyes had given her a few weeks before, the small woman used the tails of her reins to whip the black gelding on and on through the driving rain of the brewing storm. A splintered chain of deadly lightning forked down ahead of her but Squirrel Sally kept the horse moving and raced through its smoking wake. Tree stumps like tombstones were all around the charging horse and its mistress but neither gave them any thought. All the intrepid pair could see was the campsite a half-mile ahead. The huge fire that McGee and his cronies had piled high with debris and kindling was still defying the rainfall and blazing, a solitary beacon for which the young rider was aiming.

Like the man she hunted and loved there was never any fear in her heart. Never any doubt as to what course she should take. Just like Iron Eyes had done before her, Squirrel Sally aimed straight at the camp with total disregard for what dangers might be waiting for her.

The diminutive woman seemed to be glued to the saddle as she steered towards the flames and smoke of the fire, which burned on a rise just beyond a line of straight slim trees. The rain was burning her eyes but even so Sally was confident that there were no living creatures with guns hiding there.

As she drew closer to the place where so many men had died Sally leaned back and slowed her mount. When she reached the deep crater she stopped her exhausted horse and sat staring at the camp. The bodies had all gone but every hair on the nape of her slim neck told her that death had recently visited this place. It was as though she could still smell the familiar stench of death lingering on the very air itself.

Sally kicked the sides of her horse and urged it to walk up into the camp beyond the line of trees where, unknown to Sally, Iron Eyes had taken cover a few hours before.

Her hunter's eyes surveyed the area as the flickering flames lit it up. The rain had not yet washed away all the blood that had been spilled here.

Her feet did not reach the stirrups of the high saddle but it had made no difference to the youngster. Sally knew how to ride bareback and encourage a horse to find a speed most grown men could never equal, no matter how sharp their spurs were.

She guided the horse to one of the

supply wagons, then dropped to the ground and studied the side of the vehicle.

Her small hands lifted the sodden canvas tarpaulin hanging over its tailgate. The light from the campfire bathed the wooden side of the wagon in a red hue. She looked at the bullet holes and then at the crimson mess which had soaked into the planking of the prairie schooner. Her fingertips touched it and she raised them to her nose. Sally sniffed.

'Blood,' Sally said confidently. She rubbed her fingers down the front of the long wet coat. 'I sure hope it don't belong to Iron Eyes.'

She held on to the reins of the horse as another deafening explosion of thunder shook the area. The horse snorted nervously but was soon soothed by her small hands as her eyes darted and looked upward at the storm clouds.

It was like looking at living monsters as the clouds flashed and battled with one another. She returned her attention to the scene around her. The rain was steady and was becoming heavier. The worst of the storm was yet to come.

Sally pulled the collar of the coat up and fastened its top button against the night chill. She led the horse around the fire as its flames danced like a crazed sidewinder before her. The wind was getting stronger with every passing heartbeat. Soon any living thing in this land of tree stumps would be at the storm's mercy; she did not want to be here when that happened. She knew only too well what forks of lightning could do to anything on the ground.

Again she thought of the blood.

'Where are you, Iron Eyes?' Sally asked the air.

Every part of her soul and female intuition told her that Iron Eyes had been to this place. By the look of the churned-up ground a lot of other people had also been here. Even the sodden ground could not disguise the marks of more than a dozen sets of horseshoe tracks that were all around her.

Then, as a blinding series of lightning flashes stuttered and lit up the whole area Squirrel Sally saw the forest. It was the first time that she had been aware of it.

She smiled and rubbed the rain from her face.

'Bo said that Iron Eyes was headed to the forest to try and get his hands on an outlaw,' Sally muttered to herself. 'That's got to be the forest. That's got to be where my betrothed has headed.'

Her small hands gathered up the reins as she prepared to mount the high-shouldered gelding. She went to step on an empty beer keg to help her climb when she noticed something. Something that only the eyes of a hunter would have spotted.

She bent over until her nose was only a foot above the ground. Then she straightened up and swallowed hard.

'Whoever them other riders was, they all headed off in the same direction,'

Sally said. Then she stepped on to the barrel and leaped up on to her mount. She adjusted herself on her high perch, then looked down at the hoofmarks again. 'I got me a feeling that they're all on the tail of my Iron Eyes. If any of them varmints harm a hair on his head I'll make 'em pay.'

The sky rumbled as though a hundred war drums had suddenly been struck at the very same time. The air shook all around her as she dragged her rifle from the long saddle scabbard. Sally cranked its hand guard. A spent brass casing flew out as a fresh bullet was drawn up from the magazine, which went the length of the barrel. She heard the bullet find its place just under the rifle's hammer.

'Nobody hunts my man,' she growled. 'Nobody 'cept me.'

She lashed the rifle barrel back. It struck the tail of the black gelding and the animal leapt into action. Squirrel Sally clung to the fast-moving horse with her powerful knees as her hands

164

worked the reins feverishly.

Horse and mistress thundered straight towards the dark, ominous-looking forest. A forest where, her heart told her, Iron Eyes was. A forest where, her innards told her, more than a dozen horsemen had also gone.

Fearlessly the tiny female aimed the nose of her mount straight at the forest. There was no other way for people like Squirrel Sally. You always rode straight into the jaws of your enemy and hoped they choked on you.

14

The sky above the forest suddenly erupted into a dazzling and deafening display of nature's powerful fury. Forks of lightning traced and splintered in all directions as the storm clouds at last reached the remote woodland.

Kansas John Smith was true to his word and had reached the narrow trail that led to the clearing long before the severely injured bounty hunter. Leaving his horse tethered to a tree at the foot of the steep incline Smith drew his guns and made his way upward towards the clearing. It had only been a matter of weeks since Smith had last travelled by this secretive route, but it was already overgrown and slowed the gunman's pace.

Less than a hundred yards away across the clearing the weary bounty hunter reached his goal. The journey had taken its toll on the already dog-tired Iron Eyes. He was bleeding badly as he rested a hand against a tree and then somehow managed to tie his reins to its trunk.

His thin body had been torn apart by the vicious claws of the mountain lion and refused to stop pumping crimson gore from what remained of his chest. Every deep bloody gash glistened as lightning flashed far above him in the brooding sky but Iron Eyes felt no pain from his wounds. He was far beyond feeling anything now. Now the only thing the bounty hunter had left in his arsenal was his natural instinct for survival.

Yet even that was no longer as keen as usual.

Normally, when wounded, Iron Eyes would either burn the wound as he had done with the gash on his face or pour whiskey over it and then sew the skin together crudely with the large needle and catgut he always kept in his saddle-bags.

Since reaching his horse again he had done neither.

His mind was filled with a noisome fog that blurred his thoughts. There seemed to be no urgency in repairing his already scarred body, and yet in truth there was.

This was the first time he had been savaged by anything as ferocious as a puma. What Iron Eyes did not know was that the claws and fangs of a big cat were often as poisonous as the bite of a rattlesnake. Unless the deep gashes on his torso were cleaned the fog inside his skull would only get worse.

Then he would die.

He staggered away from the tree and pulled the reins free again. Like something more dead than alive Iron Eyes led the horse out into the open to where he remembered the spring and creek were situated.

He stared around him, but did not seem to be able to focus upon anything clearly. His long thin legs kept on making for where his flared nostrils could smell the water he knew his horse needed. He was like a drunken man, yet, in all his days of hard drinking, Iron Eyes had never once been able to get drunk.

The sensation bewildered the thin bounty hunter.

No amount of whiskey had ever affected him and yet the claws of the puma and the loss of so much blood was causing him to stagger like a drunkard full of rotgut. He inhaled the perfume of fresh spring water again and headed towards it.

Iron Eyes was confused. He had lost a lot of blood before but for some reason this time it was different. He had no idea that poison was surging through his body: poison that was killing him just as surely as his enemies' bullets and arrows had vainly tried to do over the years.

The clearing was big but it had seemed a lot bigger when he was young. Even so it was taking the unsteady bounty hunter what seemed a lifetime to walk across to the spring and creek.

Leading his mount behind him through the drizzling rain Iron Eyes forced himself to keep going. Then the horse's ears pricked as it heard the sound of the babbling spring. Then it too caught the smell of the water: the water it craved. The horse pulled hard on its reins. It wanted nothing more than to reach the water and drink it.

'Quit tugging, gluepot,' Iron Eyes raged as the animal kept pulling his unsteady body. 'Ya dragging my damn arm out of my sleeve.'

The horse continued to try and escape its new master and run to the precious liquid it so desired. It was far stronger than the injured bounty hunter but somehow Iron Eyes managed yet again to summon every scrap of his dwindling strength and hold on to his mount. It was not much of a horse, his dazed mind told him, but it was a horse. It had brought him into the forest and could get him out again.

'Easy, you ornery bastard,' he gasped in a rasping whisper to the thirsty mount. Then, at last, the stronger horse pulled violently on the reins in the hands of the bounty hunter. Iron Eyes staggered and then tripped. His legs gave way beneath him and Iron Eyes fell forward.

Without warning the horse bolted. With the reins wrapped around his scrawny wrist the bounty hunter was lifted off his feet and dragged across the clearing until the parched animal reached the creek's ice-cold water.

Iron Eyes lay for a few seconds beside the hoofs of the horse as it drank its fill. He raised his head and stared through his limp black hair at the fast-flowing creek only a couple of feet in front of him.

'Whiskey,' he muttered. 'I need me some whiskey.'

The dazed bounty hunter reached up and grabbed his saddle stirrup. He hauled himself back to his feet and tried to steady his shaking body as he fumbled with his saddle-bags.

Then suddenly his head filled with a white fog. It began to spin as though he were being physically swung around. He felt sick but there was nothing inside his belly but whiskey.

His fingers felt the glass of a bottle but then he toppled away from the horse. Iron Eyes was falling but there was nothing he could do to prevent it. The ice-cold water splashed high and wide as Iron Eyes landed in the creek and then sank the few inches to the riverbed.

Still gripping the long leather reins tightly in his skeletal hands, Iron Eyes sucked in water. He vainly tried to pull his head out of the creek. He was face down in the water. His head began to feel as if it were being crushed as the cold water numbed his already confused mind. Slowly the rest of his torso sank into the icy flow until only his boots and the sharp spurs were on dry land.

No matter how hard he tried Iron

Eyes could not push himself out of its shallow depth.

All Iron Eyes could do was drown.

Water filled his mouth and nostrils. He wanted to fight but there was nothing left to fight with. The horse had dragged the very last scrap of energy from his delirious body.

The horse stood beside its unconscious master and continued to drink. It had been a long time since the lathered-up animal had tasted the precious liquid it craved and it would drink its fill before raising its head.

Iron Eyes was unconscious. Totally unaware of his plight as he lay submerged beside the painted pony. A trail of diluted blood mingled with the water as his hideous wounds continued to bleed.

Suddenly, from behind some bushes, a sturdy man with a rifle held across his chest approached the drowning figure. With each step the man kept looking all around the clearing for any hint of danger.

At that same moment Kansas John Smith came crashing out of the bushes across the wide expanse of grass that lay between them. The larger man swung on his boots and levelled his rifle at the gun-toting Smith.

Both men stared at one another. Neither knew who he was looking at as lightning flashed above them and illuminated their weapons.

Each man squeezed his triggers at the same time.

Another flash of lightning above the clearing matched and bettered the brief explosion of gunplay. Fiery lead crossed the clearing in both directions as the rifle took on the handguns of Tyler McGee's right-hand man.

The sturdier man felt the heat of his opponent's bullets as they passed him but it was his Winchester that won the argument. Smith twisted and then fell into a cruel heap just after the second rifle shot tore through him.

With the echo still vibrating in his ears the other man pushed his hand guard down again and expelled the brass casing before yanking the guard back up. His eyes darted around the area as another flash of lightning gave illumination.

He spat contemptuously at the motionless body and then continued on to the creek. The sight of the bounty hunter half-submerged in water spurred the man to act.

He acted quickly. He knelt. His right hand reached down and took hold of the mane of long black hair.

With one mighty jerk of his muscular arm he hauled Iron Eyes' limp body out of the creek and dropped him on to the grass. The bedraggled bounty hunter was like a rag doll. There seemed to be no signs of life in the long thin frame.

'Iron Eyes,' the voice said knowingly. 'I thought it was your rotten, stinking carcass I spied.'

The man raised a boot, laid it in the middle of Iron Eyes' mutilated chest and pressed down. He watched as the bounty hunter's head turned and coughed out a couple of pints of bloodstained water.

'Reckon you ain't dead but you sure are chewed up,' the man said in a low, deep voice befitting his stature. 'At least the cold water has stopped them wounds in your flesh from bleeding for a while. Reckon I'd better get you home and sew you up.'

The man hung the rifle over his shoulder by its leather strap and bent down. His hands went under the skinny armpits of the still unconscious bounty hunter. He lifted the bedraggled figure off the grass as if it were almost weightless.

'Damn it all!' the surprised man said. 'I reckon you don't weigh no more than a sack of feathers.'

The burly figure retraced his steps. The horse followed, as its reins were still firmly gripped in the bony hand of the unconscious bounty hunter.

'If I had any sense I'd have let you die, Iron Eyes,' the man said as he kept walking towards a gap in the bushes.

'Trouble is, my ma never had herself any smart offspring. Nope. Not a single one with sense enough to know it don't pay to save the life of a critter hell-bent on killing you for the bounty on your head.'

Jacob 'Two Fingers' McGraw disappeared into the undergrowth still cradling his burden as though it were a sickly child.

Just as McGraw vanished from view another man came from the same narrow trail that Smith had used only moments before. Preacher Bill paused for a moment and stared down at the dead body of his cohort. The sound of the gunfire was still ringing in his ears as he reached down and searched Kansas John's pockets. He found a fat wallet and rammed it into his own shirt front.

'You won't be needing this, but don't go fretting none, Kansas,' Preacher Bill said. He cranked his Winchester's mechanism and primed its magazine. 'Like the Good Book tells us: an eye for an eye. I'll avenge you.'

Clutching his rifle across his chest, Preacher Bill bent low and strode across the clearing towards the place where he had seen the stalwart Two Fingers McGraw disappear.

He laughed to himself.

It was the same laugh he had uttered when he slew the defenceless Indian woman. It was the laugh of a madman.

15

The black gelding came to a halt as Squirrel Sally entered the dark forest for the first time. She held on to her reins and allowed her eyes to adjust to the drastic difference in the amount of light capable of penetrating the dense woodland. Then her attention was drawn to the flaming torches far above her on the high trail.

She watched as the torches vanished from view and McGee led his remaining riders towards the clearing.

'Well, that sure ain't Iron Eyes up there,' Sally said to herself. She looked all around the area in an attempt to get the lie of the land. 'He don't need no torch to get him to where he's going.'

She thought for a moment.

'They must be after my man,' she uttered as the horrifying thought overwhelmed her. 'I got me an inkling they're hunting him down. Damn it all. Hunting my beloved Iron Eyes like he was a dog.'

Sally knew she had two options.

She could either try to follow the horsemen up the perilous trail, or she could find another way up to the very top of the mountain. If she followed the riders she would always be a half-mile or so behind them, but if she could find another, faster way to the summit of the forest she could stop them before they achieved their objective.

Again she looked all around her as she tried to see if there was another route. Then she saw something which brought a smile to her handsome face.

Directly ahead of her, half-hidden by entangled vines, a couple of huge trees stood proudly. But it was not the vines nor the trees that had caught Squirrel Sally's eye. It was what lay just behind them.

Sally urged her black mount forward until it reached the trees. She leaned over the neck and head of the horse and grinned even more widely.

'That's it,' Sally said confidently. 'That's my way up to the top of this damn tree-covered anthill.'

She leaned back to the saddle-bags and flicked up one of its satchel covers. Her small hand fumbled around for a few moments, then she pulled out a long-bladed machete.

Still balanced on her saddle Squirrel Sally ran a thumb along its well-honed blade.

'This'll do just fine,' Sally said confidently. 'I sure hope old Bo don't miss it. Maybe I should have told him I was borrowing it, but he might have said no. I'd have hated to shoot that fat man again.'

The diminutive young woman balanced on top of her high-shouldered mount, and started to hack at the vines in front of her. After only three chops of the machete the obstruction fell to the ground.

Squirrel Sally stared at the waterfall. Then she tilted her head back and studied the high cascade. It looked to the youngster as though it reached the very sky itself. Sally returned the machete to the saddle-bags and unhooked the cutting-rope from the horn of her saddle. She hooked its coil over her shoulder.

'I can climb that and when I get to the top I'll be higher up there than any of them varmints.' Sally grinned with confidence and forced the horse to move closer to the never-ending flow of water. 'I'm coming, Iron Eyes. Coming to save your bacon again.'

16

Squirrel Sally fearlessly climbed the huge tree that grew beside the waterfall with all of the agility of the creature she had been named after by Iron Eyes. There was no fear or doubt in the young woman of her ability to climb the large tree with its great branches spread out in all directions. Sally had swiftly worked out that one of those branches reached to within a dozen feet or less of the top of the waterfall, where it spilled over the rocks. A cloud of vapour indicated where she had to reach and she was closing the distance on it quickly.

Sally had her trusty rifle secured to one end of the rope on the ground near her horse. The other end of the long cutting rope was tied around her slim waist. When she reached her goal she would pull the rifle up.

The ancient tree seemed to go on for ever towards the storm flashing far above her, but Sally knew where and when to halt her progress. The branch she chose to stop at was higher than the top of the waterfall opposite. She paused for only a few seconds and surveyed the top of the cliff and the cascading water that tumbled ceaselessly over its rocky lip. It was about fifteen feet from the trunk of the tree. The distance would be reduced once she ventured along the broad branch towards the place where the water noisily spilled over the rim of the rocks.

Few men would have had the courage to venture out so far above the deadly drop, but Sally gave it little thought. She knew she would not fall and that was what made the difference. It seemed to take for ever for her small hands to haul the rifle up by the rope to where she balanced. Her bare feet could feel every ridge of the rough bark beneath them. At last she had the Winchester in her grip again.

As Sally looped the rope back into a coil her eyes studied every part of the terrain around the never-ending flow of water that raced over its rim.

Even with her daredevil spirit Sally realized that leaping from the tree to reach the cliff was not something you did without considering.

A flash of lightning sent flickering light through the forest. Enough light for her to see the shine on everything that faced her. The steady flow of water over the falls and its constant cloud of vapour had made every leaf and rock wet. And wet meant slippery.

'Damn it all!' Sally cursed. 'If I land wrong I'm going to just slide off that hunk of land.'

She looked down fearlessly.

It was an awfully long way down to the pool where her horse was drinking. She rubbed her neck and looked across at the land around the falls. There was a tree a little way back from the edge of the cliff. It had branches nearly as stout as the one she was standing on. One had been broken halfway along its length. Sally knew she could rope it if her luck held out.

'That's it!' Sally snorted as she slid her rifle through her pants belt until it was firmly wedged. 'If I can lasso that critter I can swing across.'

It sounded easy.

Squirrel Sally made a loop with the rope; then she began to swing it around and around until it had momentum. This was no harder than roping a young calf, she told herself. She kept building up speed until the rope began to sing.

It was a tune Sally knew well.

With expert precision Sally released it.

She watched the rope fly across the distance between the tree branch she was balanced upon to the tree standing beyond the edge of the falls.

Her aim was true.

The loop found the broken branch. Sally jerked the rope back towards her. The rope's loop tightened.

'Got ya!' Sally smiled. 'Now, as long

as that branch ain't rotten it ought to be able to take my weight.'

The young woman gave the rope a few hearty tugs before she was confident that it was secure. Then she wrapped the rest of the cutting-rope around her slim waist again. Sally's small hands tightened the rope.

'Reckon that's it,' she muttered.

Holding on to the rope Sally ran along the branch and leapt through the rising mist. For a moment she could not see anything as her long wet hair covered her face.

Sally raised both her bare feet as she cleared the top of the waterfall. She shook the water from her face and stared wide-eyed at the tree she was approaching at speed.

She was flying.

Flying through the cold vapour and heading straight for the tree that, she now realized, was far bigger than she had at first thought, Sally readied herself.

'Holy smoke!' she managed to yell.

Squirrel Sally closed her eyes and crashed into the tree. She fell on to her back in high, lush grass that covered the creek's embankment.

The youngster lay for a while on her back, then she rubbed the blood from her nose and sat up. She blinked hard and gave out a huge smile.

'Well I'm damned. I done it.'

Sally staggered to her feet and then untied the rope from her waist. She pulled the rifle from her belt, spat at the ground, and moved away from the tree.

She knew that she had achieved her goal. She was now higher up the mountainside than any of the torch-carrying riders she had seen making their way up the narrow trail earlier.

She sniffed the air.

Forests were nothing new to her keen nostrils. She had spent her entire life hunting animals and recognized every scent that drifted on the air.

Then an even wider smile filled her handsome face.

'Iron Eyes.' Sally purred like a

triumphant kitten as she detected his unique aroma amid so many others. 'I'd know his stink any place. I could find that critter blindfolded in a barrel full of ripe skunks.'

Holding her Winchester in her left hand Sally ran across the moist terrain to where her flared nostrils told her she would find her man.

Told her she would find Iron Eyes.

A deafening thunderclap shook the forest, lightning exploded far up in the heavens above the forest. For the briefest of moments the intrepid Sally Cooke could see the clearing half a mile ahead of her through the trees.

She had never run so fast.

There had never before been any call to do so.

Now there was. Every sinew in her small body screamed at her that time was of the essence.

Sally could not afford to waste one moment of it.

17

A mile away from where Squirrel Sally had started running a small cabin stood amid the dense trees. It stood a few hundred yards away from the clearing and had been heavily camouflaged by Two Fingers McGraw in a vain attempt to conceal its existence.

Inside the cabin the bounty hunter felt hands on his scarred brow. Small delicate hands. The scent of whiskey filled his nostrils. Iron Eyes inhaled the fumes deeply. His eyes flickered and then opened.

He lay motionless on the soft cot as his vision slowly returned and the fog in his eyes cleared. He blinked hard and tried to move his brutally damaged body. The pain of the fresh stitches across his chest stopped his attempt to rise.

'Where the hell am I?' Iron Eyes

asked. He raised his arms and rubbed his eyes with his unusually clean hands.

At first he saw nothing but the dim light of a lantern that glowed somewhere above him. Then he managed to focus upon it and the roof it was suspended from.

He was in a cabin, his befuddled brain told him. How he had come there was a mystery to which he would soon discover the answer.

'Something don't add up,' Iron Eyes said. He sniffed his clean hands and inhaled the scent of soap. It was an unfamiliar scent to the bounty hunter.

He moved his head and saw the face of a child. A very young child: apparently no more than three years of age. It was a young girl with hair as black as his own. The young smile seemed neither mocking nor sympathetic.

Just curious.

The young girl smiled again and raised the hem of her shabby skirt to cover her shyness.

'Who are you?' Iron Eyes rasped. 'Are

you an angel like I've bin told about? Are you?'

Then the figure of a large man came into view just behind the little girl. His large hands rested upon her shoulders and Iron Eyes stared at them.

There were two fingers missing from the left hand.

The bounty hunter looked up at the bearded face. The man was also smiling, as though triumphant in some scheme that the injured Iron Eyes had no knowledge of.

'Her name is Alice, Iron Eyes,' McGraw said. 'She's my daughter. You could say she's an angel. She's pretty enough.'

Iron Eyes remained silent. He just watched as her tiny hand was raised and touched the far larger one of her father. Then the bounty hunter lifted his head and looked down along his naked chest. It had been sewn up as though it were saddle leather but it was now no longer bleeding. The smell of whiskey filled his nostrils.

The weary bounty hunter laid his head back upon the pillow. A thousand thoughts were spinning inside his skull but none of them made any sense any longer.

Now things had changed.

There was no longer just black and white. Now there was a spectrum of grey.

He had always lived by the rule that he hunted outlaws who were wanted dead or alive and dispatched them to their Maker but now he was confused.

How could he kill an outlaw when that same man had saved his life?

'McGraw?' Iron Eyes managed to say.

The outlaw gave a firm nod. 'Yep. You ain't mistaken. I'm Jacob McGraw.'

'Two Fingers McGraw,' the bounty hunter added.

The outlaw raised his left hand and moved it closer to Iron Eyes. 'Yep. Just like it says on the Wanted poster. I guess my missing fingers are a bit of a give-away.'

'And you knew who I was?' Iron Eyes continued to stare at the little girl. She was obviously half-Indian by her handsome looks. She was also coy but still smiling at the hideous face; it did not seem to alarm her. 'I recall falling into the creek and being too damn weak to get out. I was drowning. You must have saved my hide. Why?'

'I knew it was you,' McGraw told him. 'Right from the moment I saw you down at the loggers' campsite. I've been waiting for five years for you to turn your attention to me. It's bin a long wait.'

'Why didn't you shoot me?' Iron Eyes glanced briefly at the bearlike man, then returned his gaze to the far prettier face at the side of the cot. 'You could have picked me off clean and easy when I was down there. I saw you up in the trees. You could have ended me then and there. Why did you save my life if you figured that I was after you?'

McGraw gave a shrug. 'I could have killed you or let you drown, but I ain't no killer. Never killed nothing but game for the pot in all my days.'

'The Wanted poster tells a different story.' Iron Eyes raised a hand and traced with his fingertips the stitches that had closed the savage gashes on his chest. 'It says you are. Why else would you be wanted dead or alive?'

The burly figure gave a shrug. 'I was set up by a corrupt banker, Iron Eyes. Set up as a bank robber and killer by that varmint to cover up the fact that he'd robbed his own bank. I was a drifter who had met the banker in a saloon. I asked for a loan to tide me over until I found some work. He invited me to the bank just before closing time one night. I was allowed in and then he started shooting his tellers and told me I'd better run. So I ran and then I found out that he'd told everyone that I had killed them folks and stolen ten thousand dollars from his safe.'

Iron Eyes thought about the words. They sounded true enough, because

McGraw had proved that he was no killer by actually saving his life. No killer would ever have done that.

'Yeah. I understand. When it comes to the word of a banker against those of a drifter there's only one critter most folks would ever believe,' the bounty hunter whispered. He tilted his head at the child. 'Your pa is an honest man, Alice.'

'And a loser.' McGraw pulled a hand-carved chair to the side of the cot, sat on it and lifted his daughter up to rest on his knees. 'I've bin hiding in this forest ever since.'

'Was it you who threw my cutting-rope down that slope?'

McGraw nodded and grinned. 'Yep. I knew that you'd never climb out of there in a hundred years of trying.'

'I'm obliged.'

'How'd you feel? I washed the poison out of them cuts with some of your rye,' McGraw said. 'Sewed you up as best as I could but it would have helped if you had a tad more flesh on your bones.'

'My head is a lot clearer now,' Iron Eyes said. 'How come I was all mixed up?'

'Don't you know nothing?' McGraw sighed. 'All the big cats in the forest got poison on their claws and fangs. When that puma ripped you up the cuts were filled with it. Most animals they rip apart die soon afterwards from the poison.'

Iron Eyes could not take his eyes from the smiling child. 'Where's your ma, Alice?'

Her smile vanished. Tears filled her large eyes and she turned to sob into the capacious chest of her father. McGraw looked sternly at the long thin figure on his cot.

'She's dead, Iron Eyes,' he said.

The bounty hunter managed to raise himself up from the cot until he was in a sitting position. He did not like hearing females cry, no matter how small they were. His trembling hand reached out and touched her back.

'I'm sorry. I didn't figure on that.'

McGraw gave a slight shake of his head. 'It's still a mighty raw wound for us to cope with, Iron Eyes.'

'What happened?'

The expression on McGraw's face changed again. This time it was like stone. He was remembering and that was something he did not like doing.

'She was killed by one of the men who came into the forest to keep an eye on them lumberjacks.' McGraw said, sighing. 'There were two of them. We spotted them weeks before and we decided to keep clear of them. Then one day I was out trapping game with Alice here in the high country. When we got back I found my wife close to the clearing. She had been hurt real bad either before or after she was killed, Iron Eyes. Whoever done it took themselves a trophy.'

Iron Eyes tilted his head as he placed his boots on the earthen floor of the cabin.

'Trophy?'

McGraw inhaled deeply. His eyes

filled with tears. 'Yep. The damn killer cut himself off a chunk of my little wife. You understand? Alice ain't spoken a single word since we found her poor ma.'

Iron Eyes gave a silent nod.

He had heard of such things before but this was the first time that it had been confirmed to him. He felt sick in the pit of his stomach but tried to conceal his horror from the father and child.

After some moments the bounty hunter asked the question which was burning into his very soul.

'Do you have any idea who the critter was who murdered your wife, Two Fingers? A single clue as to his identity?'

McGraw nodded and fished out a torn page from a Bible. 'I got this, Iron Eyes. I found it clutched in my wife's hand. She must have ripped it from a Bible during the struggle.'

Iron Eyes gritted his teeth. 'That torn page fits a book that I reckon ain't too far away.'

'Do you figure he's one of them riders that trailed you into the forest?'

'It's a fair bet, *amigo*.'

Suddenly little Alice sat bolt upright and pointed at the door of the cabin. She gestured urgently. Her eyes were wide and filled with terror.

'What's wrong, Alice?' McGraw asked his daughter.

'She heard someone, Two Fingers.' Iron Eyes stood and grabbed his guns from his bloodstained trail coat at the foot of the cot. He cocked both their hammers, moved to the door and stared out through the small gap between it and the frame. 'We got us uninvited guests.'

Before McGraw could ask the tall thin man what he was thinking of doing, Iron Eyes had left the cabin and disappeared into the darkness.

The half-naked Iron Eyes moved like a phantom away from the cabin with both guns held firmly in his bony hands. McGraw had built his cabin in the perfect place, yet even so it had been discovered, he thought. The brush surrounding the small dwelling was dense until he reached a large boulder set within spitting distance of the clearing.

Lightning flashed across the sky.

Then he saw them. A dozen or so horsemen were riding beyond the trees towards him. They had their rifles drawn.

The skeletal figure dropped on to one knee and stared at the small army of ruthless riders who had taken the same route to the high country as he had.

They were following his tracks, Iron Eyes thought.

Tracks which would lead them to McGraw and the tiny Alice.

A chill swept over the kneeling hunter. It had nothing to do with the temperature. It was because he knew that these men were cut from the same cloth as the one who had murdered and mutilated the child's mother.

A fury welled up inside the bounty hunter.

He would not allow any of them to get their hands on McGraw's daughter. They had slowed their pace and the horses were walking as the lead rider surveyed the ground following the tracks left by Two Fingers and Iron Eyes' horse,

'Damn it all!' Iron Eyes cursed. 'That bunch don't know when to quit. They're as ornery as that damn mountain lion was.'

Suddenly there was a noise to his right. Iron Eyes swung on his knees and levelled both his Navy Colts at the tiny figure running straight at him.

'Iron Eyes!' Sally gasped as she came to a halt beside him. He grabbed her shirt and tugged her down. 'Hush, Squirrel. We got us a heap of trouble brewing.'

She looked at his painful chest and the fresh scar on his face and shook her head. 'What the hell happened to you?'

Iron Eyes was about to answer when he saw the riders stop their mounts and drop to the ground.

'Damn. They heard you, Squirrel.'

Sally peered through the brush at them. 'Who are they?'

'Trouble, Squirrel.' Iron Eyes snorted. 'Big trouble.'

The words had no sooner left his lips than the shooting started. Flashes of deadly lead tapered in red shafts across the forest at the pair of kneeling figures. Half a dozen bullets ricocheted off the boulder as others became embedded in the trees around them. Sally was first to return fire with her trusty rifle.

Iron Eyes eased himself up and away from his female companion and rested his shoulder against a tree. He raised both his guns and narrowed his eyes. His honed vision penetrated the gunsmoke of the advancing men.

He squeezed his triggers and watched two of Tyler McGee's hired gunmen fly up into the air as his lethal accuracy held true.

Again and again Iron Eyes hauled back his hammers on his pair of matched Colts and fired. Each time he found a target. Sally rose to her feet, turned her head and spat out a sentence which chilled the tall, thin bounty hunter.

'You stay here. I'm going to get closer.'

'No, Squirrel.' Iron Eyes watched in horror as the small youngster ran away from the safety of the boulder and vanished into the tall brush. She had not heard him above the sound of the gunfire.

Finale

The forest air was thick with gunsmoke as thunder continued to rumble far above the gunfight: gunsmoke that moved like a haunting of ghosts across the land between Iron Eyes and the enemies he could no longer see. The shooting paused for a moment. The bounty hunter cocked his hammers again, then realized that the rest of his ammunition was in the deep pockets of his trail coat back in the cabin. He quickly checked both his guns.

There was only one bullet left in each of his weapons' smoking chambers. An anticipatory chill traced his spine. He had no idea of how many of his attackers were left. No idea if two bullets would be enough to win this battle.

He rested an arm on the boulder. His eyes searched the fog of gunsmoke for a clear target. A shot echoed around the area as a hot taper cut across the air just above his head. He ducked.

This shot had come from a different direction, Iron Eyes thought. It came from his left. He twisted around and saw the elegant figure of McGee stepping away from the trees with a rifle in his grip. Smoke trailed from the Winchester's barrel as the major cocked the weapon again. The military man raised the rifle to his shoulder and aimed at his kneeling target.

McGee fired. The bullet caught the trunk of the tree next to Iron Eyes' head. Blinding splinters of sawdust showered over him. Unable to see clearly, the bounty hunter teased the trigger of the Colt in his left hand. The gun spewed out lead, which hit the ground a few feet in front of McGee.

Tyler McGee cranked the hand guard of his repeating rifle again and levelled the weapon at the momentarily distracted Iron Eyes. The kneeling man knew he had only one bullet left and had to make it count.

Both men stared at one another.

'You're going to die,' McGee said. 'You've killed all my men, whoever you are. You are most certainly going to pay dearly for that annoyance.'

The words had only just left his lips when the major was knocked violently off his feet. He crashed into the ground and lay in a lifeless heap as lightning flashed.

Confused, Iron Eyes staggered to his feet. He was about to call out to Sally when he heard twigs snapping under boots behind him. He knew that bare feet never snapped twigs, so it could not be his young female friend. This was a man.

'Drop them hoglegs,' the gruff voice ordered. 'And reach for the sky. Killing McGee has made me hanker to kill again.'

Iron Eyes dropped his guns.

'What in tarnation are you?' Preacher Bill asked the tall figure as Iron Eyes slowly turned to face the last of

McGee's men. 'You sure don't look like nothing I ever set eyes on before.'

'I'm Iron Eyes.'

'Say your prayers, Iron Eyes.' Preacher Bill grinned. 'I'm sending you back to Hell.'

'Then do it.' There was no fear in the bounty hunter's demeanour as he stared down the barrel of the rifle at the creature before him. 'I ain't feared of dying. Gotta be less painful than living.'

Preacher Bill pulled his Bible from his pocket and shook it at the defenceless man. 'Repent your sins. Repent and the good Lord will forgive you.'

Iron Eyes stared at the book. There was dried blood upon its cover. This was the killer of McGraw's wife, he realized. 'You ever kill an Injun lady in this forest? Did you?'

A hideous smile crossed the face of the preacher.

'I sure did. A worthless heathen woman,' he boasted.

Enraged, Iron Eyes was about to leap

at the creature who stood before him with a rifle in one hand and a Bible in the other when a shot rang out from behind his skeletal shoulders. He felt the heat of the bullet as it passed his naked arm and hit Preacher Bill dead centre. No sooner had the body hit the ground when Iron Eyes plucked the book from its dead fingers. He open it and saw the torn remnants of the page that McGraw had shown him.

'Good shot, Two Fingers,' Iron Eyes said.

McGraw walked to Iron Eyes and lowered his smoking rifle.

'That's the first man I ever killed.'

Iron Eyes showed him the Bible. 'It was the only one you ever had to kill, Two Fingers. That animal killed your wife.'

There was a brief silence.

'Did we win, Iron Eyes?' Sally asked as she came wading through the tall grass towards the two men. 'I got me two of the varmints over yonder.'

McGraw looked at the approaching

Sally. 'Who is she?'

Sally stood next to the tall, ravaged figure of the bounty hunter and held on to his pants pocket. 'I'll answer that. I'm his betrothed. I'm his woman.'

The burly McGraw watched as Iron Eyes looked down at the dead body of Preacher Bill. He was thoughtful. Then Iron Eyes took the rifle from the hands of the young woman and cranked its guard down and up. He aimed at the left hand of the corpse and fired twice.

'What you do that for?' Sally asked, grabbing her Winchester back. 'Why'd you shoot two of his fingers off?'

Iron Eyes looked over her head at McGraw and winked.

'Hell, Squirrel. That's Two Fingers McGraw the outlaw. I'm taking him back to collect the bounty on his stinking head.'

Sally was confused. 'But . . . ?'

McGraw patted Iron Eyes on the back. 'I'm obliged, Iron Eyes. Mighty obliged.'

'I owe you, Jacob.' Iron Eyes turned

to walk back to the cabin. He glanced back at Sally. 'Are you going to stay there catching flies or are you coming back to meet a pretty little gal named Alice?'

Squirrel Sally shook her head, shrugged and then trailed the two men. 'You got any whiskey, Iron Eyes?'

'I sure hope so, Squirrel. I sure hope so.'

THE END

We do hope that you have enjoyed reading this large print book.

Did you know that all of our titles are available for purchase?

We publish a wide range of high quality large print books including:
Romances, Mysteries, Classics
General Fiction
Non Fiction and Westerns

Special interest titles available in large print are:
The Little Oxford Dictionary
Music Book, Song Book
Hymn Book, Service Book

Also available from us courtesy of Oxford University Press:
Young Readers' Dictionary
(large print edition)
Young Readers' Thesaurus
(large print edition)

For further information or a free brochure, please contact us at:
Ulverscroft Large Print Books Ltd.,
The Green, Bradgate Road, Anstey,
Leicester, LE7 7FU, England.
Tel: (00 44) **0116 236 4325**
Fax: (00 44) **0116 234 0205**

Other titles in the
Linford Western Library:

WHIPLASH

Owen G. Irons

Sandy Rivers and two fellow trail hands were taking a well-deserved rest in the Durant saloon when the injured man staggered to their table — whipped half to death, then knifed in the back. He had come to warn them of something — but died before he could finish what he had to say . . . The knife and lash-marks appear to implicate their old trail boss Amos Coyne; when he then steals the hands' horses, stranding all three men in Durant, there's nothing for it but to se out and track him down . . .

THERE COMES AN EVIL DAY

Paul Green

Fugitive bank robber George Munro's dramatic escape from Yuma Prison was taken as a personal affront by his captor, Marshal Sean Barry. Having finally tracked his quarry down to the sleepy border town of San Tomas, Sean is disappointed to find only a grave — and the dead man's twin brother, a crusading priest. Father Joseph Munro is determined to rid San Tomas of the ex-Confederate marauders, led by the ruthless Colonel Silas Quinn, who brutally control the town. Can Sean help the cleric win his fight?

THE SUNDOWN RUN

Hank J. Kirby

Yancey Wade needed money, badly, and joining up with Frank Greer's wild bunch seemed the quickest way. But with Greer's plans to rob the Sundown Run — a legendary transport whose stagecoaches carry a fortune in gold ingots and bristle with shotgun guards — Wade soon discovers it is also the riskiest. Though many have tried, nobody has ever successfully robbed the Sundown Run before. But he has no choice — do it, or pay the ultimate price . . .

POPE'S BOUNTY

Aaron Adams

Jaded gun-for-hire Simeon Pope takes what he thinks will be a routine job. But he finds himself working for both sides of a divided family: the man who wants his errant brother disposed of, and the father who wants his prodigal son safely found . . . Confronted by a bad man, a mad man and a lawman, Pope must find a way to satisfy all his clients, impress the woman he desires — and stay on just the right side of the law.